The Bartolini Legacy

A secret, an inheritance, a journey to happy-ever-after!

A diary...

After their parents' sudden deaths, the Bartolini siblings Bianca, Gia and Enzo return home to Tuscany and discover one of them is illegitimate!

A will...

As they're reeling from the bombshell, the will is read. The luxury family estate will be left to the sibling who can generate the greatest income.

A summer to remember...

While they wait for the DNA test results, each sibling embarks on their own vision for the vineyard's future. They have six months that will take them on a journey of self-discovery and finding love along the way...

Read Bianca's story in
The Prince and the Wedding Planner

Discover Gia's story in
The CEO, the Puppy and Me

And look out for Enzo's story
Coming soon!

e of those surprises
re are others that are so
ng, that it steals your

hing to get back the
Instead, she must deal
ts, a will that has put her
and a family secret that
apart. How could her life

Moretti led a solitary
od friend led him to
vie, skyrocketing him to
en a lady sneaks onto his
mes it's a fan. However,
rying to help a puppy,
nclusions—because they
sometimes they couldn't

ollided, neither will ever
must take a journey into

The CEO, the Puppy and Me

Jennifer Faye

Puppy

Jennife

Stroka

ɔk may be used or reproduced in
en permission except in the case of
articles and reviews.

acters, places and incidents

Award-winning author **Jennifer Faye** pens fun, heartwarming contemporary romances with rugged cowboys, sexy billionaires and enchanting royalty. Internationally published, with books translated into nine languages, she is a two-time winner of the *RT Book Reviews* Reviewers' Choice Award. She has also won the CataRomance Reviewers' Choice Award, been named a Top Pick author and been nominated for numerous other awards.

Books by Jennifer Faye

Harlequin Romance

The Bartolini Legacy

The Prince and the Wedding Planner

Greek Island Brides

Carrying the Greek Tycoon's Baby
Claiming the Drakos Heir
Wearing the Greek Millionaire's Ring

The Cattaneos' Christmas Miracles

Heiress's Royal Baby Bombshell

Once Upon a Fairytale

Beauty and Her Boss
Miss White and the Seventh Heir

Snowbound with an Heiress
Her Christmas Pregnancy Surprise

Visit the Author Profile page
at Harlequin.com for more titles.

Praise for
Jennifer Faye

"Ms. Jennifer Faye always delivers the most poignant romantic stories. Romance is in the air and the ending is truly heartwarming for everyone. *Claiming the Drakos Heir* is Ms. Faye's best book, yet!"
—*Goodreads*

CHAPTER ONE

THIS WAS IT.

The moment Gia Bartolini and her two siblings, Enzo and Bianca, had been waiting for.

And yet this was also the moment they'd been dreading.

On this sunny June day, their lives were about to be once more upended. And worst of all, it could be any one of them who received the devastating news—that they were not a Bartolini.

After their parents had unexpectedly died in an auto accident a few months earlier, their lives had never been the same. Her older sister, Bianca, had found their mother's journal, which contained a secret—a big secret, a *huge* secret. Their mother had had an affair years ago, and one of the siblings wasn't a true Bartolini.

And to make matters worse, their parents had spelled out in their will that only one of them would inherit their childhood home—a vast estate and vineyard in Tuscany. The two remaining

l fortune in cash
of them wanted
til Bianca had lit-
ing. Now she was
nd that left Enzo
e out who would
me and the fam-
licated situation.

wrung her hands

credible ability to keep everything organized. Together, they kept the hotel running smoothly.

Upon Bianca's acceptance of the prince of Patazonia's marriage proposal, they all knew things would have to change once more. Bianca had to let go of her wedding planning business in order to assume her new responsibilities—first as a princess and a short time later as the queen.

Not wanting the wedding business that meant so much to her to die, she'd put her assistant, Sylvie, in charge of upcoming weddings, and Bianca flew between the vineyard and the palace on a regular basis, making sure everything in both places was running smoothly.

And then there was Enzo. He'd given up his work in France, where he'd married some of the world's finest grapes to create the most amazing wines, in order to return home and take over the Barto Vineyard. Would he regret that decision if he were not a Bartolini?

Gia's gaze moved around the room. Each sibling had consciously or unconsciously taken a seat on a different side of the room from the others. Their parents' deaths had divided the family. And Gia didn't know if they'd ever be close again.

Even though it was a summer morning, a distinct chill hung over the room. Gia folded her arms across her chest. She'd never felt so worried and—and scared. Yes, she was scared of what the DNA results would reveal. Would her family—the only family she'd ever known—be able to navigate past this?

She had absolutely no idea. Her mind was reeling with all the possible scenarios. None of them were good. All of them had heartache and pain. It wasn't right. And it was her parents' fault. They'd done this to their own children. What kind of parent held on to such an important secret for so long?

What if she wasn't a Bartolini? She quickly dismissed the idea. That couldn't be the case. Even Bianca had pointed out that Gia had been her father's favorite. It wasn't something that she would ever admit to anyone, but her father used to spend extra time with her, teaching her how to ride a horse, how to pick a grape at just the right time. When she was little, he would carry her around the vineyard on his shoulders. No matter how busy he was, he made time for her.

But that knowledge and those memories didn't lessen the significance of this moment. No matter what, three lives were about to change. And Gia didn't like change. She liked routine. She liked the reassurance of knowing what to expect. And right now, she had no idea what to expect. Would it be Bianca? Or Enzo?

Her heart went out to them. She couldn't imagine what it must be like to be facing such a great unknown. She would be there for them, doing what she could to lessen the blow. She loved her siblings with all her heart—even if things had turned turbulent lately.

But if Aldo Bartolini wasn't the biological father of one of them, who was? And why had their parents kept it a deep dark secret? The questions nagged at her.

Gia clenched her hands together, noticing a slight tremble. She wanted to stand up and tell the attorney to burn the unread DNA results— let everything go back to the way it used to be. Back to when her overprotective brother gave her dates a stern warning about dealing with him if they did anything to upset his little sister. Back to the times when she and her sister could spend hours on the phone talking about absolutely nothing in particular and yet ended up talking about everything.

"Thank you all for coming," said the attorney, Mr. Lando Caruso. The older gentleman sat behind what had been her father's desk as though it were his. "I know waiting for these results hasn't been easy. So I'll dispense with any advice except to tell you that these results in no way change the will that your parents left behind."

Gia's insides shivered with nerves. This was it. This was the last moment all three of them would

aced fingers. She
when he read the
of her siblings to
ss a Bartolini.

neet of paper. He
nd then his gaze
e's a bunch of le-
I'm sure none of
oment." He was
re we go. The lab
re indeed the bio-
rla Bartolini—"
Bianca pressed.
et's get this over

eyes, lifting

l, this wasn't her
bserver.
per, took off his
net with each of
mpathy emanat-
eared his throat.
olini sibling who

... Gia."

Mr. Lau

Gia's

This was the last

This can't be right. There has to be a mistake.

The attorney looked at her with pity. "I'm sorry, Gia."

No. No. No. This isn't happening.

And yet it was happening. To her.

She sprang out of her chair, which toppled over. She backed up, stumbling into it.

I am the outsider.

It was at that precise moment that her world came to a screeching halt. She wasn't even sure she was still breathing because the attorney's words sucked the oxygen from the room.

I'm not a Bartolini. I'm not a Bartolini.

The words swam around in her mind at a dizzying pace. Her stomach churned. She didn't move. She didn't speak. Was it possible this was just some horrific nightmare? Her gaze moved around the room. They all looked at her with pity in their eyes.

It's true. She inhaled a sob. *I'm the outsider.*

Each admittance was like a dagger to her heart. The scene before her blurred. She blinked repeatedly. How did this happen? Why her? Not that she'd wanted it to be her brother or sister either. Why did it have to happen to any of them?

The next thing she knew, Enzo and Bianca were beside her. Bianca enveloped her unmoving body in a big hug. She wasn't sure what Enzo did because she just couldn't process anything.

She vaguely heard the deep timbre of his voice. It was the words he spoke that eluded her.

I am not a Bartolini.

Her world had gotten smaller and smaller until she was caught up in her own thoughts—disturbing thoughts. Painful thoughts. Anguished thoughts.

I am not a Bartolini.

CHAPTER TWO

She wasn't a Bartolini.

Not a true Bartolini.

Not like her brother and sister.

Each time she thought of it, Gia felt betrayed. The knife of pain would sink further into her heart. How could they have kept this from her all of this time?

And who was she if she wasn't a Bartolini?

She recalled what her sister had said once about possibly not being a Bartolini, the fear she'd expressed that her father—if not Aldo—might be a criminal. Anything was possible at this point. And that made the agony that much worse.

Though her siblings tried to comfort her, she closed them out. They didn't understand this level of uncertainty—about herself, about the past and about the future.

Betrayed by the two people she thought she could trust most in the world—her parents— Gia threw up barriers around her shattered heart.

After all, who was going to care about her—to love her—when she had absolutely no idea about her true identity, her heritage?

Gia had barely slept or eaten since the DNA results had been revealed. And each day the walls of the villa felt as though they were closing in around her. She didn't belong here. But where did she belong?

Thankfully she had assistants to pick up the slack with the hotel. Right now, it took all her willpower just to take care of herself. She felt like a fraud. She wasn't Gia Bartolini any longer. But she didn't know who she was. She was a woman who'd been lied to all of her life. How could her parents have done this to her?

Anger roared through her veins. It wasn't fair that this life-altering news was tossed in her lap—destroying everything she thought she knew about herself—and her parents weren't here to explain it to her, to fill in the details.

Bianca had stuck around a couple of days, but last night she had to return to Patazonia as Prince Leo was waiting for her. Their engagement was to be made formal and their wedding date announced for December of that year. It seemed her sister was becoming the queen of planning quick weddings.

Already the mad rush to have a wedding planned by a future princess was dying off now that word was out that Bianca was no longer running the day-to-day operations, but rather overseeing things from a distance. Gia knew as time went by and her sister's calendar filled in with royal obligations that Bianca's visits to the villa would grow farther apart.

Gia was happy for her sister, but sad for herself.

It was though the rug had been pulled out from under her. And she was struggling to regain her balance, because she had nothing to grasp on to. She had no idea who her biological father was or even how to contact him.

Frustration and anger balled up in her gut. The poignant emotions clawed at the back of her throat. And then they erupted in an anguished groan.

She had taken three days to wallow in her pain, but now it was time to do something. Something good must come of this heartbreaking disaster. She refused to think this wasn't some sort of journey she was meant to go on.

That was it! She was meant to find her biological father. It would be an adventure for both of them. Because surely he didn't know about her. If he did, she imagined he would have fought to be in her life. That's what fathers did—looked out for their children. No matter what.

She had to find him. Now. This very moment. Too much time had already passed.

She jumped out of bed. Gia rushed to the shower for the first time in forty-eight hours. She wasn't going to just let this unknown past swallow her up. She would find the answers she wanted—the answers she needed.

After a quick shower and a moment to run her fingers through her short hair, fixing her pixie hairstyle, she was headed out the door of the guest house where she resided. She was a lady on a mission. She entered the main house and successfully avoided everyone as she took the back stairs to the second floor.

In her parents' room—the only bedroom she'd yet to convert to a guest room—she began her search. Sure, she and her siblings had been through this room before looking for clues, but she was certain they'd overlooked something. And she wasn't going to stop until she'd found it.

She started in one corner of the spacious room. No piece of furniture was overlooked. Every nook and cranny was examined. She had no idea how long she'd been searching by the time she'd reached halfway around the room. So far she'd uncovered absolutely nothing...

Creak.

It was the door. Gia inwardly groaned, realizing she'd forgotten to turn the lock.

"Gia?" It was her brother's voice. "What have you done?"

There was astonishment, surprise and disapproval in his voice. Like he had room to judge her. He had his life just as he'd always known it. He knew who his mother and father were. No one had lied about his birth. He knew that he'd gained his passion for growing grapes from his father.

But what did she have? A bunch of questions? An unknown—unnamed—father? No. Enzo didn't get to judge what she said and did now.

She straightened, leveled her shoulders and turned to her brother. "I'm looking for answers."

He stepped farther into the room. "But this?"

So she'd made a little mess. She'd clean it up. She turned to see what he was complaining about. And then she realized it was more than a little mess.

She'd removed every drawer from the dresser and flipped it over to see if there were any pages, documents or scraps of paper taped to the bottom that might point her in the right direction. She'd moved furniture, looking beneath each piece with the flashlight app on her phone as well as searching for loose floorboards where things might be stashed.

So far all she'd succeeded in doing was making a mess. But it wouldn't stop her. If it took pulling up each and every floorboard or chipping away at any uneven surface on the wall or ceiling, she'd do that too. She wasn't leaving here without something to point her in the direction of her biological father.

"If you've come here to stop me," she said, "you can just turn around and leave."

Enzo didn't say a word at first. "I didn't come to stop you. I came to help you."

Disbelief quickly followed by a rush of love flooded her system. "You did?"

He nodded. "I'd be doing the exact same thing if I were you. Just tell me where to start."

She turned all around, looking for a clean space for him to start in. And then she pointed to the vanity—the place where her mother would powder her nose and apply her eye shadow each morning. "Try searching there."

Enzo nodded and set to work.

Together they worked side by side just like they always had. But did Enzo still consider her as much his sister as he did before the test results? She didn't know. And she didn't have the courage to ask. Some things were better left unsaid.

"I've got something!" Enzo held up a black leather-bound journal.

"Where was it?"

"There was a secret compartment in the back of one of the drawers. I'm afraid that since I didn't have the key, I had to break the drawer."

"Who cares?" She rushed forward and took the journal from him.

She flipped opened the book to a random page, immediately recognizing her mother's handwriting. At last she would learn the truth.

But would she like what she'd learn?

CHAPTER THREE

IN HIS OFFICE on the small Italian island of Lapri, Riccardo Moretti pressed enter on the computer keyboard. Then he typed the last lines of coding for a cutting-edge predictive algorithm. It would streamline transportation, pointing out inefficiencies as well as suggesting alternatives.

He smiled. If this worked out the way he'd planned, not only would he make a nice tidy profit, but more importantly it would also help reroute food and supplies to those in need. Shipping costs would be minimized and absorbed by transportation companies instead of charitable organizations and private donors. This program could make a fundamental difference in people's lives.

Buzz. Buzz.

He pressed the intercom button to speak with his assistant. "Yes, Marta."

"Sir, there's a woman on the other line. She's calling about your uncle's house."

"My uncle?" Uncle Giuseppe had passed close to a year ago, leaving his entire estate to Ric.

"Yes, sir. It sounds serious."

Alarm shot through him. He knew possessing a now vacant house might cause some security issues, but he wasn't ready to part with it. For some reason he wasn't willing to examine too closely, he had an attachment to the place.

Ric checked his cell phone. There hadn't been any alerts from the alarm system. How could that be?

Still, he didn't have time for problems. There were only a couple of hours before his very important business dinner—a meeting that had taken months to arrange. But he couldn't just ignore this call. "Put her through."

He'd speak to the woman. Surely it was nothing important. And then he'd be back on track. Everything would work out.

In no time, an older woman came on the phone. "Ric, is that you?"

He smiled, remembering his uncle's neighbor, the kindly woman who'd offered him cookies still warm from the oven when he was young. "Mrs. Russo?"

"Yes. It's me. Pardon me for bothering you at the office, but I thought you'd want to know there's a young woman snooping around your uncle's house."

"Is she trying to break in?"

"I don't think so. But I can't be sure. She's moved to the back, and I can't see her now."

His office wasn't far away. "I'll be right there."

And with that he ended the call. He rushed to his car, anxious to catch this intruder. He wanted to stop them from doing any damage to his uncle's estate.

He went to call the police but then hesitated. Calling them would draw media attention, and he'd had more than his share in recent weeks. He'd check out the situation and then decide if the authorities needed to be called in.

In no time, his midnight blue sporty coupe rolled to a stop in front of the house. From the front, nothing looked disturbed.

However, Mrs. Russo had indicated the person was making her way around the house. Being that it was quite a large place, he would need to make the rounds in order to surmise if the intruder was still there.

He stepped out of his car. Immediately, Mrs. Russo came rushing out of her house. He waved her off, signaling for her to go back inside until he had the situation under control.

It could be as simple as a salesperson, but then why would they have ventured around the house? Ric moved carefully and quietly. He wasn't about to engage the intruder if they were armed. But that didn't mean he couldn't witness what they were up to so he could report it to the police.

As he neared the back of the house, he noticed a young woman in a flowy white-and-aqua top. White capris clung to her curves and a coordinating purse completed the summer outfit. As his gaze lowered, he noticed she only wore one high heel. As she hopped around on one foot, he noticed the other aqua heel, which appeared to be stuck between two cobblestones.

Her face was turned away from him. She had short, dark, spiky hair. If she was a burglar, she was an awful one. First, that summer outfit was bright and eye-catching. And those shoes, wow, how could anyone walk in them? Well, obviously she couldn't, or she wouldn't be hopping around on one foot. Whoever this woman was, she certainly seemed quite harmless.

Ric stepped into the backyard. "What are you doing here?"

The woman's head turned. Her eyes rounded. Her mouth opened, and for a moment nothing came out. "I…uh, heard something back here."

"Heard what?" He crossed his arms over his chest as he waited for her to explain herself.

He'd been down this road before. Beautiful women made up every excuse possible to access his home or the office. One had even posed as he problem

hunched down, trying to free her other shoe. Seriously, how did he end up in these situations?

The whine sounded again.

He moved to help the woman first.

"No." She shook her head. "I'll get this. Go help him."

Ric found a new appreciation for the woman, more worried about her pet than herself. He looked around but couldn't see the animal. He wasn't even sure about the size of the dog, but it couldn't be very big or he would have spotted it by now.

Still, it would just take a moment for him to help the woman. He bent over and pulled on the heel. To his surprise, it was thoroughly wedged in there. She really was in a bit of a bind.

He pulled on one of the stones with one hand while working the shoe free with the other. And then it pulled loose. When he handed it over, he waited for her to have a meltdown about the mangled shoe, but she quietly slipped it back on her foot.

He felt compelled to say something. "Sorry about the shoe."

"It's okay. It's kind of the way my life has been going lately." When she put weight on her foot, her face scrunched up into a look of discomfort. She immediately raised her foot again.

"What's the matter?" he asked.

"I twisted my ankle when my shoe got stuck. It's not a big deal. Just help the puppy."

"You're sure?"

"Positive."

He did as she asked. However, his light gray loafers weren't the best shoes to venture through this overgrown jungle either. Limbs poked and prodded him.

There went the high-pitched whine again.

"Do you see it?" the woman asked.

He shushed her as he backtracked a bit. And then he followed the scratching sound to the back corner of the garden. There were shrubs and other overgrown vegetation blocking his view.

He worked his way through the vines, ignoring how the thorns dug at his arms. As the dog whimpered, Ric grew more determined to help it, even if he ruined his clothes during the rescue.

And then at last, he spotted a little puppy all caught up in some old wire. Its big brown eyes turned to him. They showed its panicked state.

"It's okay." Ric spoke in a calm, soothing tone. Every time the puppy got worked up and yanked to get loose, the wire dug farther into its flesh. Ric knelt in front of it. "I'm going to help you."

The puppy stopped wiggling for a moment and studied Ric. The animal watched his every movement but didn't react. It was either so relieved to finally have help or it was too exhausted to put up much of a fight. Either way, it took a bit but Ric was able to untangle the dog. He made a mental note to call a gardener ASAP. This place not only looked bad, but it was also dangerous to anything that meandered in here. He didn't want any other creature getting hurt.

But the deepening red stain on the dog's ginger fur had him concerned. Heedless of the blood and dirt, Ric scooped the pup up and held it against his chest.

"It's okay," he said in a gentle voice. "You're safe now."

He made his way back along the overgrown path to where the woman was standing. He stopped in front of her. "Here's your dog."

All her attention was focused on the animal. However, she made no motion to take it from him. That was strange.

"It's not mine." And then her eyes widened with concern. "It's hurt."

"I know. It got caught up in some wiring. Looked like some old fencing or something." He glanced at the dog wiggling in his arms. It was still bleeding, and it was getting all over his shirt. "Could you hold him?"

"Sure." They moved carefully, trying to avoid aggravating its injury.

Ric pulled off his ruined shirt. In any other context, the surprised look on the woman's pretty face would make him laugh but not now—not under these circumstances. "It's for the puppy, to help stop the bleeding. I have another shirt in my car."

The woman's glossy lips formed an O.

Once the shirt was securely tied around the dog's midsection, it settled in her arms. "Does he belong to one of your neighbors?" she asked.

"I don't know. It's not my…" He was going to say it wasn't his house, but that was no longer true. It was his house—his great big house. That he had absolutely no idea what to do with.

It was far too big for just him, but he didn't have the heart to get rid of the place where he'd spent so much time with his aunt and uncle when he was little. It was the only real home he'd ever known. The short time he'd lived with his mother, they'd moved from one house to the next. His jaw tightened as he slammed the door on the unhappy memories.

Ric turned his attention back to the villa. He supposed he'd have to work up the nerve to cut the emotional ties and sell it sooner rather than later. There was no point of letting it turn to rubble because he couldn't bear to part with it. After all, he was a businessman. He made tough decisions every day. Why was this one so much harder than the rest?

That he couldn't answer. Maybe it's what he

was waiting for—the answer. And then he could move on.

"Your shirt will help for now," she said, drawing him from his thoughts. "But we have to get him to a vet. The cut looks bad. It might need stitches."

We? When had they become a we?

When Ric finished adjusting the makeshift bandage, his gaze met the woman's. She was no longer frowning at him. "I take it you approve?"

Her gaze lowered to his chest before her eyes quickly rose to meet his. Color bloomed in her cheeks. "I… I do. Now, where's the closest vet?"

"I have no idea. I don't have a pet." For a man used to having all the answers, he felt totally out of his depth here. And he didn't like the feeling—not at all.

"If you hold him again, I can look on my phone."

Noticing that the puppy looked content in her arms, Ric shook his head as he pulled out his own phone. "I'll do it."

In no time, he had the address of the first listed vet. It was across town. He thought of calling for an appointment, but that would just waste time, and by the way the blood was soaking the makeshift bandage, they didn't have time to wait. The puppy needed help now.

He read off the address to her. "I would just show up. I'm sure they'll help you."

"Help me?" Her gaze searched his.

It was then that he really looked at her, taking in her spiky, short hairdo and those vivid blue eyes. He'd never seen eyes of that vibrant color. They were stunning, just like the rest of her.

She frowned at him. Oops. He'd missed something she'd said, but he refused to let on that he'd gotten utterly distracted.

"You want me to go with you?" he asked, hoping he was on the right track.

"Well, this is your home, is it not?"

He thought of his afternoon appointments. His calendar was full. But more importantly, he had that meeting with Giovanni Grosso. This was the man who held the keys to Ric's company expanding into charitable work—a can't-miss opportunity.

But then Ric's gaze moved to the puppy. It needed help, and it did get hurt on his property.

With a resigned sigh, Ric nodded. "We better hurry."

He would call his assistant on the way. Hopefully, his appointment with Mr. Grosso could be moved around. He knew the man was only in town for a short period.

The woman limped along beside him. He felt bad for her.

"Do you need some help?" When she sent him a puzzled look, he added, "You know, walking?"

She shook her head. "I'm fine. I just sprained it. It'll be better in no time."

They rounded the house, and he came to a stop next to his car. He reached in the open window for his gym bag. He withdrew a muscle tee and pulled it on.

Ric turned back to the woman. "Do you want to lead? Or follow?"

"I... I don't have a car."

Interesting. But there was no time for questions—even if he had a lot of them. He opened the passenger door. "Hop in."

She did so without argument.

Once they were on the road, he realized he had absolutely no idea what this woman's name was. They'd been thrust into saving the puppy and had dispensed with the pleasantries. But if they were going to help the puppy—together—they should at least exchange names.

"We didn't introduce ourselves," he said. "My name's Riccardo Moretti. You can call me Ric."

"My name's Gia."

No last name. Interesting. He supposed he didn't blame her for being a bit reserved. After all, she didn't know him at all.

When he glanced her way, he found her head turned to the side as she stared out the window.

So much for making small talk. Besides, he preferred the silence. He wasn't one to get close to people. After his mother dumped him on his aunt and uncle at the age of seven, he'd learned not to trust people. And the fact his mother never told him who his father was only added to his distrust—distrust that morphed into anger. Not knowing how to deal with such strong emotions at such a young age, it came out at all the wrong times.

It wasn't until he was older that a teacher took him under his wing. Mr. Rinaldi told him that he should take all the energy he put into being mad at everyone and use it to make a difference in the world. He had to admit that his fourteen-year-old mind didn't think the man knew what he was talking about, but when he began applying himself to his classes, just to see if he could do it, he was quite surprised with how easy mathematics and computer sciences came to him. And soon he was at the top of his class—for the first time in his life. When he realized the only thing holding him back was himself, he excelled at most anything he tried.

Ric swore to himself that he was never going to need anyone again. He built his life so that he could be totally autonomous. He lived his life behind a computer screen. He ordered food, clothes and anything else without the need to interact with people. He would never be let down, used or hurt again.

Minutes later they arrived at a very busy veterinarian's office. Thankfully, the staff took notice of the severity of the cut and rushed them back to an exam room.

While Gia was inside, seeing that the dog was properly taken care of, he moved outside. He phoned his assistant, trying to figure out how to reorganize his afternoon.

When Ric ended the call, he heard the office door behind him open. He turned to find Gia limping toward him with the puppy in her arms. It now had a red collar and a matching leash. "How'd it go?"

"They said the cut looked worse than it was. The vet put in stitches and gave me some medicine. And a cone. They also supplied me with a care package of food and toys to tide us over until we get to the pet store." Gia lowered a big white bag from her shoulder and handed it to Ric. "Poor guy. We're good to go."

He was relieved to hear it was nothing more serious than stitches. "I'll just go inside and pay."

"I already took care of it."

"You did?" He could tell by the frown on her face that it was the wrong thing to say. He'd been caught off guard as he was used to always picking up the bill.

"I did."

"They also checked him for a chip," she said. "He doesn't have one. They took his photo and said they'd post a notice for a lost dog."

"That's a good idea. I'll post a notice online when I get home."

Once Ric got Gia and her bundle situated in the passenger seat, he closed the door. He rounded the car, hopped in and started the engine. At last he could get some answers that had been nagging him since he'd found the woman in the garden.

But first there was something he had to know. "Where can I drop you?"

She mentioned a trendy little hotel in the heart of Palmas. "But I don't think it allows pets."

He grabbed his phone and checked. She was right. He smothered a sigh. Whatever could go wrong with this day had gone wrong.

"We'll just have to find a place for the puppy," he said.

"You could take him." Her eyes held a hopeful gleam.

Ric shook his head. "I'm never home. And I know next to nothing about animals."

"It isn't that hard. And we can't just drop him anywhere. We have to see that he gets his medicine and make sure he doesn't rip out his stitches. The vet also said we had to watch for signs of an infection."

It looked like it was up to one of them to look after the puppy until they could find its owner. But with the future of his company in the balance, it couldn't be him.

Ric shifted the car into drive. "We'll stop and pick up your things. Then we'll find you a pet-friendly place to stay."

He waited for her to argue. But instead, she nodded.

As he made his way into traffic, the questions that had been nagging him returned. Keeping his eyes on the road, he asked, "What were you doing at the house?"

She didn't say anything at first. He was beginning to think she wasn't going to answer the question. Did she have something to hide? Was she in fact one of those women who sought him out because of his five minutes of fame?

He halted that thought. Sure, he hadn't known Gia for more than an hour or so, but in that time, he'd learned a lot about her. She loved animals. She was more concerned about the puppy than her sprained ankle. And he sensed she was a good person.

She didn't strike him as the type to track him down…for what? A photo? To ask him out? He never was sure what women wanted from him. Whatever it was, they weren't going to get it. He had his priorities aligned. And they didn't allow room for him to get distracted.

Then Gia's soft voice filled the car. "I'm not really sure why I was there."

That was not the response he was expecting. "Are you lost?"

"No. Not exactly."

She wasn't making a whole lot of sense. "There had to be some reason you were at that particular house and not somewhere else."

"The address was on a slip of paper I found in my mother's journal."

If he was confused before, he was even more so now. "So you were searching for your mother?"

"No." When he pulled to a stop at an intersection, he chanced a glance at her. She once more had her head turned away. "I was searching for my father."

That answer startled him. It took him by surprise to the point where he sat motionless until a car honked behind them, spurring him into pressing the accelerator once more. His thoughts raced as he tried to put what she'd said into perspective.

He swallowed hard. "You think your father lived in that house?" She didn't answer, so he looked her way again. She nodded and he continued. "I take it that it's been a while since you've seen your father."

"I… I, uh, never met him."

Alarm bells were going off in Ric's head. Was it possible this gorgeous woman sitting next to him was his cousin? He shifted in his seat, leaving a little more space between them. This day had definitely taken some unexpected twists and turns. None of which he'd seen coming. Not at all.

CHAPTER FOUR

WHAT WAS WRONG with her?

Why was she telling this perfect stranger about the most painful secret in her life?

Gia leaned her head back against the black leather headrest, holding the puppy that was still groggy from the sedative the vet had given it in order to put in the stitches. Her fingers brushed gently over its downy soft fur. The action gave her some sort of comfort, but not enough to keep her from dwelling over the disappointment of not finding the answers she'd been seeking. If her father had ever been in that house, he was long gone now.

How was she going to find him? Was she even on the right track? The questions swirled in her mind at a nauseous pace. Maybe some people would say it didn't matter. But to her, it mattered very much.

She wanted to know, did the smattering of freckles over her nose came from him? Did he love snack food as much as her? Did he sing in the shower? They would have such a good time answering each other's questions. In no time, they'd be the best of friends. If only she could track him down.

And in the next breath, she had to ask herself if this mission would be so important if she hadn't just lost her mother and the man whom she'd always thought of as her father in a sudden and horrific car accident. No, she didn't have to stew over it or debate the matter. She knew finding her biological father would be important no matter what.

But her mother hadn't left many clues. She rarely mentioned the man in her journal, and never by name. Gia wondered if it had something to do with her father... No, the man who'd raised her. Aldo never struck her as the jealous type, but she supposed if your wife had an affair and a baby from said affair, that might make a person jealous—very jealous. Still, Aldo never let on—at least not in front of her.

So who was her biological father? And when she did find him, what if he wanted nothing to do with her? The breath hitched in her throat. It was nice to dream of him welcoming her with open arms, but what if he refused to acknowledge her?

Her pulse raced. Her throat tightened.

That won't happen. Just think positive. It will all work out. It has to.

She needed it to.

She swallowed hard. This subject was so difficult for her, but she couldn't give up now. "Have you owned the house long?"

Ric continued to stare straight ahead at the thickening traffic. "No."

That was it? A one-word answer. Not good enough. "Did you know the previous owner? Maybe he's who I'm looking for."

Ric was quiet for a moment as though debating his answer. "The house belonged to my aunt and uncle."

"Oh." Her mind ran with the idea. If the house belonged to his aunt and uncle. And if his uncle was her father—

Her thoughts screeched to a halt. No wonder he was acting strangely around her.

"Do you think— I mean, is it possible…could it be—"

"That we're cousins? I don't think so." His tone was firm.

"But we could be…"

Ric wheeled off into a parking spot and turned to her. "Did you hear about my uncle's death? Are you here for the inheritance because if you are—"

"I'm not!" She glared at him. He had absolutely no idea what she'd been going through ever since her parents died and left their family totally upended. "I swear. I have money of my own. Enough that I never have to work again if I choose not to."

"But you work now?" His tone had changed to something less hostile.

"I do. I started a boutique hotel." She didn't offer him more details than that. At this point, he hadn't earned her openness about her parents' will or the contest to gain control over the Bartolini estate.

Surprise and…was that respect flickered in his eyes? "So if I check, I'll find that you aren't some scam artist or anything nefarious?"

There he went again, ruining their semi-truce. "Check if you must, but you won't find any of those things." And then turning the tables on him, even though she knew exactly who he was from all the media hype, she asked, "And if I were to check on you, what would I find?"

"That's a good question. I'm not sure either of us would like what the media's printing about me these days." And with that he made his way back into traffic. "I guess we have things to learn about each other."

"And whether we're cousins. Or not?"

The words hung in the air between them like some ominous cloud. The potential for it to be true bothered Gia. Her cousin should not be so dashingly good-looking. The memory of his tanned, toned abs came to mind. She definitely shouldn't notice his good looks. But it was impossible not to.

Without another word, he made his way to her hotel. When he pulled up in front, he turned to her. "I don't have time to care for an injured puppy. And you can't take him into the hotel, so it looks like we're going to have to work together. Do you think we can do that, you know, for the good of the dog?"

"I don't see why not." Her gaze met his. Every time he stared into her eyes, like he was doing now, her heart raced. She swallowed hard, trying to maintain her composure. "I don't mind doing my part, but you should know I can't take care of an injured dog full-time. I'm only here for a brief amount of time. And I have things to do."

He looked as though he was going to say something, but he paused as though rethinking what he'd been about to say. "Understood."

Using the utmost care, she handed him the puppy. And then she got out. She headed into the hotel to see if they would make an exception to their no pets policy and, as expected, they refused. And so she checked out early. She wasn't sure where she was going to stay that night, but she couldn't just abandon the puppy, and Ric didn't seem comfortable caring for him.

As she made her way to her room to gather her things, she couldn't stop thinking about Ric. She'd recognized him right away in the garden. Someone would have to live under a rock not to recognize the man after all the media coverage he'd garnered for his part in that movie—this year's smash hit.

The funny thing was that he didn't have an actual part—at least not a speaking part. It was more like he came walking out of the ocean with waves breaking behind him as rivulets of water raced down from his short dark hair to his broad shoulders to his muscled chest, and then there were those six-pack abs. She could now testify that those close-ups were most assuredly real and not airbrushed.

But the fact there was a possibility he was her cousin utterly blew up all of those totally inappropriate thoughts. She'd been eager to learn about her other family, but she hadn't thought she'd end up with Ric Moretti for a cousin.

This day had started so promising.

And with each passing hour, his optimism had faded away.

A frown pulled at Ric's mouth. The fact Gia could be his cousin shouldn't bother him. After all, it wasn't like he would be upset about losing the inheritance. To be honest, he'd amassed his own fortune with his innovations. And now he wanted to pay it forward—to leave this world a little better than he'd found it.

The dog whined, drawing Ric from his thoughts. He adjusted his hold. His thumb stroked the pup's fur, feeling its little ribs in the process. This little guy had been on his own for a while now. Ric knew how that felt, but it didn't make it better. In fact, it made it worse.

"Don't worry fella. We'll make sure you end up in a good home where you'll always have plenty to eat, a warm bed and you'll never get hurt again."

The puppy turned its head and rested it on Ric's forearm. He seemed quite content on his lap. And though Ric would not admit it to anyone, he was content holding the little guy. He could see why people had pets. Although he wasn't changing his mind about walking through this life alone. No matter how cute the puppy was or how appealing it would be to share life's burdens, he knew relying on someone—trusting someone—came with risks. And he'd already paid dearly. It was a lesson he'd never repeat.

So while the puppy closed its eyes, seemingly content to fall asleep, Ric used his free hand to start searching for a hotel in the city that accepted pets. His first three tries failed.

But the more he thought about it, the more he realized the answer was right under his nose. Or in this case, the answer was right under his roof. His apartment had a spare room that had never been used. And he didn't mind having the dog there—on a temporary basis.

And it would help to have Gia under the same roof until he unraveled the real story about her. Was she really his cousin? Or was she scheming for the inheritance?

He didn't want her to disappear until he knew the absolute truth. And so the decision was made. He would offer her a place to stay.

The car door opened. Gia leaned inside. "I think we have a problem."

He smothered a sigh. "What is it?"

"It's my luggage. It's not going to fit in your car."

Why hadn't he thought of that?

The puppy sat up. He lifted his head and licked Ric's cheek. That was why he hadn't been thinking clearly. This dog had upended his entire day.

"Leave your luggage with the valet. I'll send a car to pick it up."

She hesitated, not moving. The look on her face said she wasn't sure about this arrangement.

"It'll be fine," he said. "Just give them my name."

"Okay."

A few minutes later, she returned to the car. "You were right. Once I mentioned your name, there was no problem. You must have a lot of pull in this town."

"I don't know about a lot, but enough." He went to hand over the puppy, but its little paws went into overdrive as it fought to stay on Ric's lap.

"I think he likes you." Gia smiled.

Her face glowed bright like the sun. The way her lush lips lifted at the corners to the way her cheeks puffed up and her eyes sparkled, it chased away the dark clouds that had been dogging him all day. In fact, her sunny disposition warmed a spot in his chest. He was inclined to smile back, which wasn't like him, but he resisted the urge.

Ric cleared his throat. "Who? The concierge?"

Gia laughed. "No. The puppy. Well, I don't know about the concierge," she said in a teasing manner. "Would you like me to go back and ask?"

"No." Now with the puppy on Gia's lap, Ric checked his side mirror and then stepped on the accelerator.

"Where are we headed?"

"That's what I wanted to talk to you about. I did some searching and tried to find an available hotel on the island that accepts pets, but it wasn't as easy as I would have hoped."

"Oh."

He glanced over, catching the smile slipping from her face. "But I do have a solution."

"I'm listening."

He drew in a deep breath. He knew once he uttered the words, there'd be no taking them back. "You could stay at my place. I have an extra bedroom. And it's right here in the city, so you'd be close to everything." Upon realizing that he was actually trying to talk her into this arrangement, he stopped himself. He would not beg. No way.

"I don't know. You don't exactly seem like the dog type."

He cast a sideways glance at the puppy, who was watching him. "We can manage."

"I... I don't know." She seemed genuinely caught off guard. If this was a performance for his sake, she deserved an award.

She wouldn't be the first person to try to scam him out of his money—not that his uncle's estate was truly his, at least it didn't feel that way. It felt odd to take what once had been his uncle's.

"It'll make life easier with the dog. And I have a housekeeper who stops in every other day. I'm sure she won't mind helping out with him." He wasn't so sure of that, but he would definitely make it worth her time to puppy-sit.

a sideways

feel respon-
"

; though she
e was once
. would have
gement, but
m up on the

y tomorrow,
:akes a dog."
ng. "Sounds
ιe apartment

. This whole
esence was a
his home to
she wanted
?

ιe light mid-
"

:h him." He
✓ weren't far

time is any

She had him there. He couldn't even throw out that he was on the verge of making a valuable contribution to mankind because he frankly didn't know if his plan was going to work out. Perhaps it was time to get to know his new roommate a little better. He didn't like it, but he could work from home that day—or rather what was left of his day.

"Okay," he said as he wheeled the car into his reserved spot, "I'll stay home too."

"Wait. What?"

"It sounded like you were worried about being home alone with the dog, so I'll work from home today. But this evening I have to go out."

Her fine brows rose in question, but as though she'd caught herself, she glanced down at the pup. "And if I want to go out?"

He shrugged. "I'm not going to stop you." Did she want him to? With most of the women in his past, they would have wanted him to make a fuss. But with Gia, he had the feeling she wasn't the clingy type. She had other priorities on her mind. "You can come and go as you please. I'm just sticking around today to help you out."

"You mean to help the dog."

"Yeah, that too."

She didn't look too pleased with him. He wasn't sure what he was saying wrong, but obviously it was something. The truth was, he wasn't well-versed in making casual conversation with women. Sure, he had his share of dates, but they were usually out in public. And when they were alone, conversation hadn't been foremost on his mind.

So maybe he was a bit rusty with what to say and do. Which was yet another reason he should go to the office. But he'd said he'd stay home today, and that was what he intended to do. Everything he needed to access for his dinner meeting could be done remotely.

Gia's blue gaze met his. "Would you mind getting the door while I hold on to the puppy? I don't want him jumping out of my arms."

"Sure." He hurried around the front of the car and opened her door for her. "Why don't I show you inside, and then I'll come back for the supplies?"

She nodded. "It has been a long day."

"Did you just arrive in Lapri today?"

"Yes. It's my first visit to the island. After checking in at the hotel, your uncle's villa was my next stop."

"Then you can get the puppy situated and rest while I take care of a few things."

What was wrong with him? He didn't normally play the congenial host—in fact, he didn't play any sort of host. He didn't like people invading his personal space. The only reason he had a housekeeper was because his dislike of cleaning surpassed his dislike of sharing his space.

It had actually worked out for him because Mrs. Rossi was excellent at her job. She cooked for him a couple of times a week, leaving the food in the fridge. And she was always gone before he returned from the office. Of course, that was because he would get lost in his work and forget the time until it was very late.

But having Gia and the puppy here was really going to take some adjusting for him. Still, it would give him a chance to disprove her belief that his uncle might be her father. Because Ric did not believe it. Not a chance.

Or was it that he didn't want to believe it? As she passed him and entered the apartment, he inhaled the gentlest floral scent. It teased him, drawing him in for a closer, much deeper whiff. He resisted the urge. Barely.

now her and her siblings' home—was downright warm and cozy.

How did someone live like this? She wasn't exactly a slob, but even her place wasn't this clean and perfectly arranged. Perhaps this wasn't his place. Maybe he was just borrowing it? Maybe it was part of a hotel suite plan. Yes, that sounded like a viable option.

"Make yourself at home," her host said.

"Uh, thank you." She wasn't sure how to be at home when she felt as though the apartment was staged for a photo op. "Do you spend much time here?"

She shouldn't have asked. It was none of her business. But curiosity was eating at her. She wasn't sure how to make herself at home if he really was some sort of neat freak.

Please say it isn't so.

"I spend a lot of time at the office. But I make it here at some point in the evening."

"Really?" She bit back her bottom lip, hoping to hold in any other unwise comments.

"Yes, really." His dark brows drew together as he studied her. "May I get you a drink?"

She shook her head, not trusting her mouth as it kept betraying her at every turn. There was something about being close to Mr. Tall, Tanned and Toned that disengaged her mind from her

The frustration glinted in his eyes. But even he couldn't definitively reject the possibility that his uncle was her father.

Ric sighed. "You aren't going to give up on this, are you?"

"No." There was a firmness in her voice. She wanted him to take her seriously. He had no idea how hard this was for her.

Not so long ago, she'd had a family. A mother, father and two siblings. And now it'd all been shattered. She needed to find the truth about herself—about the past. It was the only way she could move forward.

"Why is this so important to you?"

"Really? You don't think it's important to know who your father is?"

"Yes." He drew in a deep breath. "I meant, why now? Why not seek him out years ago? I mean, the timing would make anyone wonder."

"The timing?"

"Yes. You know my uncle passed away and you're looking to challenge his will."

She ground her back teeth together as heated words clogged the back of her throat.

Never speak in the heat of the moment.

Her mother's sage advice filled her mind.

How dare he think she was some gold digger here to steal his money? She liked him much better when he was just a really hunky guy on the big screen with no shirt—ripped abs on display and his mouth closed.

"You might be used to dealing with gold diggers, but I am not one." That was it. She was done with him. She gently picked up the puppy.

"You're leaving?"

"Looks that way. This was a mistake. I'll take care of the dog. Don't worry."

Without waiting for him to say a word, she turned and headed for the door. He was a stranger—a famous stranger but still a stranger. And now she was certain she didn't want to know him. And she certainly didn't want to share her painful secret with him.

"I'm sorry," he said softly. When she didn't stop—when she grasped the door handle—he said louder, "Hey! Did you hear me? I'm sorry."

She paused with one arm around the dog and her other hand on the handle. Apologies were easy. Why should she believe him? It was best they end their brief encounter now.

"I'm not used to having people in my home—in my space," he said. "And I spend most of my time at the office working so my social skills may be a bit rusty. Can we start over?"

He was trying, she'd give him that. But even so, she wasn't willing to open up about how her family had been blown apart by a devastating secret.

But she also sensed how hard that apology was for him. And it deserved a response because those manners her mother taught her at a young age, well, they were still a part of her—even if she didn't know who she truly was.

Gia turned back to him. "Apology accepted."

A small smile pulled at the corners of his lips. He went from being incredibly handsome to incredibly sexy in zero point six seconds. Gia's heart stumbled.

And then she realized she was smiling back at him. How was that possible? One moment, she was furious with him. And then the next, she's smiling at him like some lovesick teenager.

She pressed her lips into a firm line. "I should be going."

"Don't. I mean, stay. I shouldn't have been so blunt." He at least had the decency to look contrite. She supposed that was something.

"You were being honest." Now that she'd cooled down a little, she could see his perspective. It wasn't like he knew her at all. She was a perfect stranger. A rich man like himself was probably used to people trying to take advantage of him. But she wasn't one of those people.

Just then the puppy whimpered.

"I better take him out." And with that she made a hasty exit.

Luckily, there was a small park just across the

street and down the road a little way. She and the puppy were there in minutes. There were a few benches. Nothing fancy, but she wasn't the only one there with her dog. It seemed to be a popular spot.

Now what was she going to do? Return to the apartment and a man who unnerved her with his sexy good looks? Or just head off on her own?

That went wrong.

Completely wrong.

And now he'd run her off. That hadn't been his intent. Well, maybe it had been at first, when he thought she was a con artist. But he saw the pain in her eyes when he'd accused her. That sort of pain couldn't be faked. It was real. And he was the one who had caused it. He felt awful.

He started for the door. When he realized he was chasing after her, it startled him. He didn't chase after women. If anything, it was the other way around, especially lately because of that silly movie. Seriously, it wasn't even fifteen minutes of fame. It was more like sixty seconds. And it was never supposed to amount to anything. And yet it had gained so much media attention.

Ric stopped himself as he reached the door. Maybe it was best that he let her go. After all, she wasn't going to be related to his uncle. He was as certain of that as he was his name.

And now Gia was one more complication he didn't need—didn't want. He knew the dangers of letting someone into his life. When they found something better, they moved on—no hesitations, no apologies. He refused to let himself be vulnerable again.

She would find her own way—or she wouldn't. He knew something about attempting to track down missing parents. You didn't always get the result you wanted.

He turned and headed for the kitchen. He didn't know why. It wasn't like he was hungry. Still, he opened the fridge and stared inside. Nothing appealed to him.

He wondered what Gia would do for dinner. It wasn't like she could just stroll into a restaurant with a dog. Again, not his worry.

He closed the fridge and then opened a drawer with a stack of takeout menus. Some of them had worn edges. His gaze scanned the first menu. Not even his most indulgent selections could tempt him today—

Buzz. Buzz.

The doorbell drew his attention. He slipped the menus back in the drawer. So she'd changed her mind. Interesting.

His steps were swift. He swung the door open, about to greet her with some glib comment but the words died in the back of his throat. It wasn't cknowledge

s chest.

d white suit

e expecting

c could see

d his mind.

, but he had

ked like the

e the door."

nan and the

somely, the

ria's things.

What was it

ered his life

straightforward. Relationships were messy and complicated.

Even when people said they loved you, they ended up hurting you. Not that he loved Gia. He didn't even know her. And that was the whole point—he didn't want to get to know her, to let her into his world. He was better off on his own.

And with that in mind, he reached for his phone. He flipped the leather tag on a piece of luggage and snapped a photo of her name and address. His assistant was good at locating people as well as things. He was certain Marta would be able to reunite Ms. Bartolini with her luggage.

As though his thoughts had summoned her, his phone rang. His assistant's name popped up on the caller ID. She was probably wondering what was keeping him.

"Hello."

"Mr. Moretti, I'm sorry to disturb you, but I've just had a phone call I thought you would want to know about immediately."

Marta was very good at her job and dealing with people. She was used to prioritizing interruptions and only bothering him with the most important items. He had a sinking feeling he wasn't going to like what she had to say.

"What is it?" he asked hesitantly.

"Your dinner meeting with Mr. Grosso has been canceled."

"Canceled?" That couldn't be right. "You mean rescheduled."

"No, sir. His assistant called and canceled the meeting."

Ric's body tensed. This wasn't good—not good at all. He had his entire rollout planned. He was ready to start testing on Mr. Grosso's system.

"What did he say?" Ric's voice came out in a heated rush. "There has to be a reason. I want to know what it is."

Marta was quiet for a moment.

He drew in a deep breath, calming himself. "I'm sorry. I don't mean to take this out on you. I just can't believe after months of going back and forth, trying to arrange this meeting that it has fallen through."

"I'm sorry, sir. I know how much you were counting on this."

"Did they give any hints of what went wrong?"

"The assistant said that Mr. Grosso had looked over the proposal and decided there wasn't enough evidence the program works."

Ric muttered under his breath as he raked his fingers through his hair. "Of course it works. I've been perfecting it for the past year."

He wanted to say that if this man wasn't interested, he would just sell his technology to someone else, but there was no one else with pockets as deep as Grosso Global Transports. And he'd written the algorithm with that company and its needs in mind.

"What shall I do, sir?"

He wished he had a quick answer. He wanted to say to call them back—to insist on the meeting—but he knew that wouldn't work. Mr. Grosso was a recluse. The fact he'd been granted the meeting in the first place had been a miracle. But Ric wasn't giving up. He just needed a moment to regroup.

"I'll let you know." And with that they concluded their call.

He'd totally lost his appetite now. He headed out the door and straight to his car. He jumped in, fired up the engine and set off toward the office. Soon his fingers would be moving over the keyboard, and then the tense muscles in his neck and shoulders would loosen. His pounding headache would subside and he'd be able to think of a plan B.

He pulled to a stop at the next intersection. As he waited his turn to proceed, he glanced around, taking in the busy storefronts to his right. He'd moved back to the island of Lapri close to four years ago. In all that time, he'd not so much as strolled down the sidewalk. Even though most people walked or rode a moped, he always drove, no matter where he went.

Time was money. And money was power. He

e. He had a life plan—to

could thank his mother
hat it meant to do what-
your goals—even tossing
hild or leaving him home
e. The clincher had been
t she was going on vaca-
h his aunt and uncle and
he truth was, she had no
ck for him—ever. She'd

zeroing in on a small park. It was really no bigger than a few benches, a swing set and a fountain.

Today it seemed rather busy with people walking their dogs—another thing he didn't have in his life. Sometimes he thought it might be nice to have a pet, a dog loyal to him that would never reject him or use him for its own greedy needs.

And then other days, he enjoyed his freedom to come and go as he pleased. Not to have to worry about anyone else but himself. He realized how selfish that sounded, but he wasn't hurting anyone. It was simply his choice to live alone—

Wait.

A flash of bright aqua caught his attention.

Is that Gia?

He stared over at the park. The woman had her back to him, but it sure looked like her. And then his gaze lowered to the puppy with the plastic cone around his neck. It was definitely her.

Honk! Honk!

The angry horn blast reminded Ric that traffic was stacking up behind him. He proceeded through the intersection. He found a safe place to turn around, and then he backtracked to the park.

He told himself it was the luggage that had him seeking Gia. It couldn't be anything else. After all, her problems were just that—her problems.

And he had enough of his own problems at the moment.

Still, that didn't keep him from pulling into a parking spot along the road. He told himself the sooner the luggage was gone, the sooner any thought of Gia would be gone and the sooner his life would return to normal.

He climbed out of his car and headed for Gia, who was talking to an older woman. He found that odd, considering she said she was from the mainland. And she'd acted as though she hadn't been to Lapri before now. Perhaps she hadn't been telling him the truth. It wouldn't be the first time a woman had lied to him.

He cleared his throat. "Excuse me. Gia?"

Both women turned to him. The older woman with short, silver hair smiled at him. A big bright smile lit up her eyes. She adjusted her black-rimmed glasses as though to get a better look. "Aren't you?" She snapped her fingers as though she couldn't quite place the face with a name. "You know, the guy in the movie." Color rushed to her cheeks. "The one who walks out of the ocean with all of that water rushing down over that muscular chest?"

The woman certainly didn't shy away from matters. He could respect that. However, he didn't return the woman's smile. "That would be me."

"Oh, my! Wait until the women in my apartment building hear about this. I'll be the most popular person today."

Hmm…so he was only good for one day's worth of popularity. He stifled a laugh. If he'd have known the notoriety that clip would have given him, he never would have agreed to it. Still, this woman looked mighty pleased with herself—as though she'd discovered him.

Gia tilted her chin upward. There was no sign of a smile on her face. "What are you doing here?"

"I wanted to let you know your luggage has been delivered."

"Oh."

That was it? He stopped to let her know—to let her retrieve her things from his place. "I'm headed to the office, but I can let you in the apartment to get your stuff."

The older woman lightly elbowed Gia. "If I was you, I'd definitely stay." She glanced at Ric and waggled her brows before turning back to Gia. "You'll be okay with this one?"

"I will."

"Then I'll be going. I can't wait to tell Josephine about this. She's always bragging about her nephew's celebrity friends. This will get her." Then a worried look came over the older woman's face, and she turned to Ric. "You don't know Josephine, do you?"

He shook his head. "I don't know any Josephine."

"Good. Good." She turned back to Gia. "I'll see you tomorrow, if you decide to stay." Then she gave the leash in her hand a gentle tug. "Come on, Princess. It's time to go home."

And then they were alone, except for the dozen or so other people in the park. He shifted his weight from one foot to the other, not sure what to say. Still, he couldn't stand here all day. Even the dog agreed as he sat down in front of them and stared up as though asking what they were going to do now.

Ric told himself to make a clean break. He once again reminded himself that her problems weren't his problems. But he knew what it was like to wonder about a missing parent. The only problem was he didn't have a clue who his father might be. Unlike Gia, his mother didn't have a clue. When he'd asked her, she'd told him that his father was a nobody and that she didn't recall his name. Who didn't recall the name of someone they procreated with? Every time he thought of her casual response, his blood pressure shot up at least twenty points.

When he glanced around, he noticed people were pointing in his direction. Oh, no. It appeared Gia's new friend wasn't the only one to recognize him. He inwardly groaned.

"We should go," Ric said.

"Back to your uncle's place?" Hope shone in her eyes.

"You really believe he's your father, don't you?"

She lifted her shoulder before letting it fall back in place. "If he isn't, I have to believe there's some sort of link in the house."

"And if I refuse you access?"

Her pointed stare met his. "I will find out the truth. With or without your help."

He knew she meant it. And he respected her determination. He just hoped it'd be enough for her to find the answers she so desperately needed.

Ric checked the time. It was past lunch, and with his business dinner canceled, he had no pressing appointments. "Why don't you come back to the apartment? Maybe tomorrow I could help you with your search."

Why in the world had he gone and offered to help? To clear his uncle's name, sure. But when she turned to him with excitement and appreciation gleaming in her eyes, he knew there was no way he could take it back.

And yet the smile that followed sent his heart racing. And then without thinking, he smiled back. Once he realized the affect she had over him, he glanced away.

He cleared his suddenly dry throat. "Shall we go?"

"Yes."

As they walked to his car, he assured himself that her stay would be brief. He'd make sure of it—even if he had to spend every waking moment disproving her claim.

CHAPTER SIX

RIC TURNED OUT to be a surprisingly good host.

They'd even gone on a shopping spree at a pet store after leaving the park. Gia told herself accepting his invitation to stay at his apartment was the simplest solution as far as the puppy was concerned. And there was Ric's sincerity when he'd said he would help her search for her father. How could she turn him down?

After all, she didn't have any leads other than the address of his uncle's island villa. There had to be a reason her mother held on to that address. And Gia had to hope it had something to do with her conception. Because if it didn't, she might never find the answers she so desperately needed.

And so the next day, Gia stood behind Ric as he unlocked the massive door to the villa. The puppy continually barked, pulling on the leash to get away. What was up with that? Usually he was quiet—well, as quiet as a puppy could get.

Gia gently pulled on the leash. "Gin, enough."

"Gin?"

She glanced at Ric wearing an amused look. "I couldn't keep calling him puppy, could I? What kind of name is that? And he is a ginger. So I shortened it to Gin." She glanced down at the puppy. "You like your name, huh?"

Gin looked up at her as though trying to tell her something.

"Do you need a little walk?" She turned to Ric. "We'll be right back."

She let Gin lead her to the patch of grass, but instead of stopping to do his business, he pulled hard on the leash trying to get to the backyard. Gia knew the dangerous mess that awaited them back there. Gin barked repeatedly.

"No. We're not going back there." Not in the mood to fight with the dog, she leaned down and picked him up.

Her action startled Gin into silence. As she headed back up the steps to where Ric was waiting for them, Gin licked her cheek. All was well in the world once more. Well, sort of. At least where the puppy was concerned.

But now she had bigger matters on her mind. Her heart raced as she thought how this moment might lead to answers about the past—about her conception. She couldn't wait to track down her biological father.

"Please excuse the condition of the place." Ric

opened the door. "I've had it locked up since my uncle's passing. I... I just needed time to deal with it."

"I understand." Not everyone was thrust into action by a contest written into a will, like she and her siblings had been after their parents' unexpected deaths.

Gin wiggled in her arms. With the door shut, she put the little guy down to explore, but she didn't let him off the leash.

Her thoughts turned to her family's villa in the rolling hills of Tuscany. Guilt niggled her for just up and leaving the whole business with her two managers. But she just couldn't stay there and continue to act like nothing had happened.

Finding out she wasn't a Bartolini had been devastating. She'd lost her footing, and she didn't know if she'd ever feel sure and confident again—not until she found out exactly who she was and who her ancestors were. And most of all, she had to learn why her parents had lied to her all her life. Who did something like that?

"Gia?" Ric turned to her from where he now stood across the spacious foyer. "Are you coming?"

The puppy pulled on the leash, anxious to follow Ric. In comparison to her childhood home, this place was colder and a lot more proper. She glanced around, finding what looked to be expensive works of art on the walls.

While the puppy sniffed his way around the room, Gia took in her surroundings. She wasn't sure what she'd been expecting. It was as though the house was just waiting for someone to walk in the door and bring it back to life. There weren't any dust covers, though the place could definitely use them.

"My uncle's study is this way." Ric headed toward the back of the house.

She followed him. All the while, she took in the high ceilings with their ornate plasterwork as well as the collection of artwork. It was like walking through a museum. She couldn't believe Ric had closed up this place instead of moving in.

Though maybe it was the old-world style of the home that kept Ric away. After all, his apartment was state-of-the-art, and the style had a modern industrial flair to it. Very different from this villa that was from another century.

Gia entered the study, noticing all its dark wood and antiques. It was an organized room. Everything appeared to be in its spot, but coated with an inch of dust.

However in a matter of minutes, Ric had undone all the order as he opened drawers and piled papers on the desk and more on the coffee table that sat in front of the brown leather couch beneath the windows.

Gia sneezed.

Gin sneezed.

"Sorry," Ric said. "I guess it's been a while since this place was dusted."

"Can I help you go through the papers?" She wasn't quite sure what he was searching for other than proof she wasn't his uncle's daughter.

She couldn't really blame him. She knew how devastating family secrets could be. They didn't just change the past, but they also changed the here and now. And who knew about the future. Something told Gia that no matter who her biological father turned out to be, her family would never be the same. The thought weighed heavy on her heart.

"Give me a second." He heaved another stack of file folders onto the already crowded desk. "On second thought, give me a few minutes to figure out where to start looking for clues."

She wanted to ignore him and just dive into the files. She was so anxious to find the pieces of the puzzle to complete her life's story, but she had to wait. She was here at Ric's invitation. She didn't doubt if she got pushy, he'd withdraw his help immediately. She just had to be patient. That was easier said than done.

But if Ric's uncle was her father, that meant this villa was a piece of her past. And without anything better to do, why not explore the place? Maybe she would learn more about the man. The thought appealed to her.

"Do you mind if I look around?"

Ric glanced up from an open folder. He looked confused at first, as though he'd forgotten that she was still in the room. "Um, sure. Yeah. I'll be here if you need me."

And so she was off, Gin right at her heels. She hoped while she was gone that Ric would find the answers she so anxiously wanted. The home was quite spacious, with three floors of elaborately decorated rooms.

Gia noticed there were portraits of the same woman on each floor. They must be images of Ric's aunt. She had been a beautiful woman. And as Gia passed through room after room, it was obvious Ric's uncle loved and missed his wife after her passing, because her feminine touch was in each room as though he was just waiting for her to return.

Gia fell in love with the home. Its classic decor was tasteful but not overdone. And sure, it needed some updates, but whoever lived in this house next would be fortunate. She could imagine many happy family moments spent here.

Ric's image flashed in her mind. Would he someday give up his bachelor pad and settle down here? Something told her that he'd only do it once he had a family of his own. The thought dampened her mood.

She told herself the reason it bothered her was

that she still had no idea about her other family. And she had no idea why her parents had strived to keep the secret from her. Why do that? It wasn't like her parents were super secretive people. But when it came to her birth, there was a reason they didn't ever let on. Did her very existence threaten their marriage? Did they fear she would bring her biological father into their lives and it would ruin the reconciliation they'd strived to achieve?

And without knowing about the circumstances of her conception, how could she move forward? What would people think when she said she didn't know who her father was? How would anyone truly love her when she didn't truly know herself?

"Gia!" Ric's voice echoed through the wide hallways and up the grand staircase. "Gia, come here."

She left her troubled thoughts behind as she rushed down the wide staircase to the main floor and to the study where Ric was rifling through a large stack of papers. He was certainly intent on finding the answer of her paternity.

What a mess!

And he was only making it worse. But it had to be done eventually.

Ric leaned back in the old leather office chair that his uncle used to spend most of his day in before his death. When Ric was young, he imagined himself one day sitting in it and working at this very desk.

It was amazing how things had changed. Now, Ric knew he'd never live in this house. And he would never spend his days working behind this desk. It just wasn't in the cards for him.

This sprawling villa was for a family—something he'd never have. To live here, he'd be reminded every day that he was alone. But he also knew too well that people could tell you they loved you in one breath and leave you in the next. Family life was not for him. Gia may want to expand her family but not him. He was fine alone.

Ric frowned as he glanced at the overflowing desk drawers. He shouldn't have put off cleaning out the house. Not only did he have the unruly garden to tend to, but the inside would need a cleaning crew if he was ever going to make it presentable for a buyer. But those were problems for him to deal with another day.

However, he realized if he had taken the time to clean out the house, he would have found this information sooner. Realizing he'd paused, he continued scanning the page before him.

"What is it?" Gia's voice cut through his thoughts. "What did you find?"

There it was again. The hope in her voice. She wanted Uncle Giuseppe to be her father. She wanted this to be her reality. And suddenly Ric felt guilty for being right.

He cleared his throat. "My uncle saved everything. And when I say everything, I mean it. It's going to take forever to sort through all these papers."

She moved over next to Ric on the couch. In that moment, he was tempted to turn to her—to take her in his arms and kiss her.

He halted his runaway thoughts. What in the world was wrong with him? He barely knew her—though that had never stopped him in the past. And she would probably be leaving town after he confirmed his suspicion—though her imminent departure was more of a reason for him to get involved. He was torn between his rising desires and his common sense.

Stay focused. Tell her the truth. And then walk away.

He focused on the papers in his hands. "What is your birth date?"

She told him.

"So that would mean at the time of your conception my uncle didn't own this house. He was, in fact, working in New York City."

"That can't be right." She frowned.

"It is. I checked three times." He handed her the documents to see for herself. "I'm sorry."

Gia's fine brows drew together as she scanned

the very old pay statements from his uncle's employer as well as the sales agreement for the house. There was no way she could claim they were forged. Those papers were so old and aged that they'd fall apart if anyone were to tamper with them.

Maybe his uncle being a bit of a hoarder wasn't such a bad thing. Still, Ric was going to have to go through this stuff page by page. He didn't relish the idea. And he wasn't taking this mess to his apartment. No way. He'd sort through it here with a paper shredder and a very large garbage can—or two.

Gia was quiet for a long time. She must have had her heart set on finding answers today. He told himself not to get drawn in. It wasn't any of his business.

And then he made the mistake of looking at her. The pain and disappointment in her big blue eyes was like a kick in the gut. He understood her turmoil. He'd tried for years to search for his mysterious biological father. With his mother unable or refusing to help, there were no other leads for him to follow.

Gia glanced down, staring at the pages in her hand. She flipped through the papers. Her gaze quickly scanned for something.

"What's the matter?" he asked.

"The ink is faded on this sheet. I'm trying to

figure out who sold your uncle this property."
Lines of frustration formed on her beautiful face.

"Here. Let me take a look."

She hesitated as though unwilling to admit defeat but then she handed him the pages. He looked through them and noticed how some of the corners had fallen off or had been torn off. And he couldn't read the faded type print.

"I'm sorry. I can't make it out either," he said.

Gia lifted her head. Her eyes were misty. "I should have known it wouldn't be easy. Nothing about this entire journey has been easy."

The unshed tears shimmering in her eyes tugged at the walls around his heart. He reached out and squeezed her arm. "It's going to be okay. You're going to be okay. Even if you never find him, you are strong and you'll find a way to make peace with it—"

She pulled away from his touch. "How do you know that?" Anger and pain vibrated in her voice. "You have no idea what I'm going through. No one knows."

He didn't know if he should remain quiet or if he should speak up. It wasn't like he ever talked about it, though it was no secret. "I don't know my father either. I have absolutely no idea who he is or anything about him. And trust me, I did everything I could think of to find him."

Her eyes widened. For a moment, she didn't

ong time ago.

ll me either. Well, I obvi-

a father, but she refused

e gave himself a mental

out me. I hope you're not

thing for a moment as

over. "It's okay. I'll find

you'll be heading home."

ve elated him. It didn't,

o. I'm not done here."

s address in her journal.

on. And I'm not leaving

ed here at the time of my

of his neck. "What hap-

able to get the answers

'm not giving up. I have

d to Ric. "Don't you see?

v about me."

"Because if he did, he'd have come to find me."

Ric wasn't so sure that was the case, but the hope in Gia's eyes kept him from vocalizing his doubts. She'd already had enough disappointment for today. But then again, just because he'd had a disappointing journey searching for a missing parent didn't mean Gia's journey would yield similar results.

Feeling himself being drawn further into Gia's troubles, Ric stood. "I should clean up these papers before we leave."

Gia handed him back the documents, and he returned them to the big wall safe that was crammed full of information. Then he swung the heavy door closed. Safe for another day.

When he turned around, he found Gia had gathered all the folders scattered over the coffee table. He hadn't had a chance to go through them because they hadn't been labeled as anything he thought would reveal information related to the time period surrounding Gia's birth.

He noticed she had opened a folder to replace something that had fallen out. Her eyes widened as she pulled out a drawing. Her gaze turned to him. "Did you draw this?"

He shook his head. "I don't draw."

"But this looks like you might have done it when you were a kid. I think this is your name at the bottom."

He moved to the couch. He took the drawing and stared at it. He didn't recall it. But when he peered at the bottom right corner, he found his name penciled in childlike writing.

He couldn't believe his uncle had kept this. Why would he do that? His uncle never seemed that interested in his schoolwork other than making sure he got his homework done.

"Look," Gia said, "there's more of it. This folder is filled." She checked another. "So is this one. And this one."

Ric was left speechless, and that didn't happen often. After all these years thinking his uncle had been indifferent to him, Ric was deeply touched that his uncle had kept all of this stuff.

He started sorting through the folders, finding all sorts of things he'd done in school. And then they uncovered a folder with his accomplishments as an adult, including every press release since the launch of his company. It was all there. And Ric had to blink a few times. Stupid dust.

"I had no idea he kept all of this stuff."

"He loved you a lot."

A rebuttal rushed to the tip of Ric's tongue, but then his gaze moved over all the papers in front of him. Art projects to term papers to newspaper clippings. It was like a synopsis of his life. How could he deny his uncle cared for him when the evidence was staring him in the face?

"I had no idea." His voice was so soft it was like a whisper.

Gia rubbed his back as though in comfort. His instinct was to pull away. He wasn't used to anyone comforting him. But he liked her touch. He found himself welcoming her gentle concern as he took in this monumental realization.

"I was so wrong about him," Ric said. "How did I not know any of this? I thought I was a bother—a nuisance. And worst of all, I never got to tell him how much I appreciated him always being there for me—no matter what. I... I never told him that I loved him."

Gia's hand moved to his shoulder and squeezed. "He knew."

Ric wanted to believe her—he really did—but he wasn't so sure.

CHAPTER SEVEN

THINGS HAD WORKED out for Ric.

Gia was happy for him to have proof of his uncle's love.

But what about her? She let out a deep sigh. Where was her rainbow?

The following day, Gia took a moment to feel sorry for herself. Then she straightened her shoulders. Her father, um, Aldo, had taught her not to be a quitter.

Nothing good came to those who quit.

If Ric's uncle wasn't her father, she would find out who lived in the house before him. She was close—very close. She could feel it.

And then there'd be a happy reunion. Reunion? Was that the right word? After all, they hadn't actually ever met. Had they?

No, of course not. Fathers didn't just let go of their children, never to see them again. She imagined a man with the same shade of brown hair as her own, much taller than her and wearing a warm smile as he enveloped her in a big hug. Because he'd be overjoyed to know her. He had to be. Anything else—it was unacceptable. Just the thought of being rejected by her own flesh and blood…

No. It won't happen. Everything is going to work out.

The buzz of her phone halted her thoughts. Gia moved across her spacious bedroom to retrieve it from the bedside table. She glanced at the screen, finding a message from Enzo.

When are you coming home? The hotel reservations have declined dramatically. We're in trouble. You need to fix this.

He'd been trying to reach her since last night, and she'd been dodging his phone calls. The hotel was in trouble. But Gia knew if she took the call that she'd be obligated to return to Tuscany to try to fix the problem, something she couldn't do until she learned the truth about her birth. Usually she put family first, but in this moment, she needed to put herself first.

She knew that made her selfish and she felt awful about it, but if their parents hadn't kept this huge secret, she wouldn't be searching for her biological father. If there was anyone to blame for this mess, it was them. And worst of all, they weren't even here to explain any of this to her.

And right now, she desperately needed her mother. She needed to hear her soft, comforting voice. She needed her to say everything would be all right.

Gia's vision blurred as she stared at the phone. She blinked repeatedly. She would keep it together. She wasn't a crier. She was strong.

Her fingers hovered over the phone. And then she started to type.

Michael and Rosa have this. Don't worry. Everything will work out...

She reread what she'd written. Would everything work out? She wasn't so sure about that anymore. Too much had happened to continue being a Pollyanna.

She knew no matter what she said, it wouldn't be the end of the discussion. Her brother hadn't wanted her to go on this trip. He wouldn't give up until she was on a plane home. And so she deleted the message.

Knock. Knock.

"Gia?"

It was Ric. He'd promised to help her track down the prior owner of the villa. Maybe she would have news for her brother soon.

"Coming."

She took one last glance in the mirror. She ran her fingers over her hair, smoothing a flyaway strand or two. And then she glanced down to find Gin staring up at her as though questioning what she was doing.

She realized she was nervous. She wanted to look her best for Ric. There wasn't anything wrong with that, was there? She applied some lip gloss, and then she was ready.

When she glanced down once more, Gin was still giving her a questioning look, making her feel paranoid that she was trying too hard to impress Ric.

"Stop looking at me like that."

The puppy whined.

"Did you say something?" Ric called through the door.

"Um…" She rushed over and opened it. "I was just telling Gin that we were leaving."

Ric's gaze moved to the dog, who rushed over and propped himself against Ric's leg. He bent down and picked up the dog. "And how's Gin this morning?"

Arff!

Ric laughed. "That good, huh?"

"Someone has you wrapped around his paw," Gia teased.

ı. "I think you must be

th surprise. "Good one.
. us both over."

dy to go?"

m missing work. "You
rary and the courthouse

ure? Never. I'm curious
y of the house."

you can use it when you

to me, but now that you
is interesting, sure, why

ked. She didn't like the
hy should she care what
?

it was a piece of his past
searching for her past
things would be differ-
uld uncover the key to
lead her in the right di-
in her bones.

thouse were at the cen-

rtment.

walk. With the housekeeper watching Gin, they set off on the beautiful sunny day. The light sea breeze made the summer day quite comfortable. Plus, Gia wanted a chance to take in more of the old-world city.

The only disappointing part was having to switch from her pretty pink-and-white heels that matched her white skirt and pink top so well to a pair of sneakers. At least her sneakers were white with pink and yellow flowers. She couldn't help it; she like coordinated, colorful outfits. They helped her feel more confident. And today she needed a boost to get through this challenging period.

She turned her thoughts to more serious matters. What would happen after she located her father? Would he invite her to move in with him so they could get to know each other? There was no making up for all the years they'd been robbed of, but they had the here and now. They *would* make the most of it. Excitement and nervousness fought for room in her chest.

As they continued to walk, Ric informed her that there was an ordinance requiring new architecture to be approved by the city council so it didn't conflict with the older structures. Thus, the city looked as though it were from another era. Gia immediately fell in love with it. It was like stepping back in time. That was until you had a look at the pedestrians with their smart phones. It was quite the contrast. Still, she wouldn't change any of it.

She snapped some photos with her phone and then sent them off to her sister. She missed her siblings—even if she wasn't ready to go home. Not yet. Not without answers.

A message dinged on her phone. It was from Bianca.

Thank goodness. We've been wondering if we'd ever hear from you.

Sorry. I just need some time to do this on my own.

Gia's thoughts turned to Ric. Maybe not exactly on her own, but she wasn't ready to tell her sister about Ric.

Everything is good. Tell Enzo not to worry. I just need some space.

Have you found your father?

Not yet.

Gia had to keep glancing up to make sure she didn't run into anyone or walk into a lamppost.

But soon.

Is there anything I can do?

Talk to Enzo. Let him know I'm okay. But I can't come home yet.

I'll try. He's worried about you. We both are.

I love you.

I love you too.

Gia slipped her phone back in her purse.

"Everything okay?" Ric's voice drew her from her thoughts.

"Um…yes. It was just my sister. She hadn't heard from me in a while and was worried."

"I'm surprised she isn't here with you."

Gia shrugged. "It's complicated."

"How so?" When she didn't immediately answer, he said, "Sorry. I shouldn't have asked."

She shook her head. "It's okay. I've certainly insinuated myself into your life."

"You had a reason," he said. "You thought I could help you figure out your past."

"Sadly, we aren't related." She glanced his way. "Or perhaps we're lucky the way things worked out."

What had she gone and said that for? Heat rushed to her cheeks. She was flirting with him?

She pressed her lips together before she could say more.

"Maybe you're right. Otherwise it'd be quite inappropriate if I were to, say, kiss you."

"You want to kiss me?" There she went again, saying the wrong things. She should have pretended that she hadn't heard him, but how did you pretend you didn't hear something like that?

They were alone on a side street when Ric stopped and turned to her. "Would you like me to kiss you?"

Yes!

She struggled to hold back her answer.

Their gazes met and held. There was definite interest reflected in his eyes. "It sounds like you're the one with kissing on your mind."

A deep growl rattled in his throat. "I have a whole lot more than kissing on my mind."

She hadn't been expecting him to say that. His words melted her insides into a heated ball of need. Would it be wrong if she were to fall into his arms right now?

She stifled a frustrated sigh. Probably. She couldn't—she wouldn't—be one of those women who threw themselves at him.

But would that be so bad? After all, he was the one who had opened this door. Or had she? Either way, she was more than willing to yank that door wide open and march right through the opening and into his arms—

"You're smiling," he said, cutting right through her daydream. "Must mean you like the idea."

Oh, yes, she did. A car honk from farther down the block startled her back to reality. The voice of reason reminded her that they weren't out and about on this gorgeous sunny morning to fall in love. Wait. Where had that thought come from?

She swallowed hard. She was not falling for him. No way. Admiring his sexy good looks was one thing, but anything beyond that was off-limits. Because no one could truly love her until she knew the truth about herself. She reinforced the walls around her heart with sheer determination.

She wouldn't let herself be vulnerable again. Not even for someone as kind and amazing as Ric. Because whenever she found her father—whoever it might be—she couldn't stand for Ric to look at her differently, to push her away.

In that moment she knew the flirting had to stop. She straightened her shoulders and lifted her chin to look into his dark and mysterious eyes, but then she realized her mistake as her movements had only succeeded in bringing her closer—much closer—to his tempting lips.

If she were to lean forward ever so slightly, their lips would meet. And then she'd lean into his arms. He'd pull her closer. And as his mouth moved over hers, they'd get lost in the moment.

Desire flashed in his eyes. Did he know she was fantasizing about him—wanting him? Her heart hitched in her chest.

No. No. No! Get a grip girl. You are here on a mission. Don't get sidetracked.

She stifled a frustrated sigh. Was it wrong that she wanted both? A summer fling with Ric and to be united with her father. Probably. One couldn't be greedy.

Stay focused.

With great reluctance, she pulled back. "We should keep going."

He hesitated for a moment, but when she moved past him to continue down the sidewalk, he fell in step beside her. All the while, she couldn't help wondering what would have happened if she had given in to her desires and kissed him back there. Where would things have gone between them?

And when it was over, what would happen? Would she just be one more conquest for him? After all, he could practically have his pick of women. There were certainly enough of them willing to be with him.

She didn't like the thought of just being another notch on his bedpost. And she didn't like the thought of him turning to another woman with that devilish grin that made his eyes twinkle with unspoken promises of passion.

But there was no point dwelling on it. She wasn't in Lapri for fun and romance. She was here to find out who she was and get to know her father—a father who'd been kept from her. She had to right the past before she could contemplate the future.

The old book had been searched.

Every entry regarding his uncle's house had been analyzed for clues.

And they were still no closer to locating Gia's biological father.

"I'm sorry," Ric said. All the while his mind raced, searching for something they'd missed.

Deep sadness filled Gia's eyes. "This isn't supposed to be this hard."

"I don't know what to tell you. It doesn't appear the prior owner has any living relatives."

"But how am I supposed to find my father? I just know he was in that house. It's the only reason my mother would have that address in her journal on the page that speaks of him."

A woman working at the counter gave them dirty looks for making noise. Even though this was a government office, it was much like a library where speaking was frowned upon.

"Come on," he said. "Let's get out of here."

Gia didn't argue. They returned all the research material they'd borrowed and headed out the door. The bright cheery sunshine seemed to mock the dark stormy look on Gia's face. Right about now, he'd be willing to do most anything to put the smile back on her face. But even he couldn't work miracles. He'd already run an exhaustive search on the internet for any reference to a man who might fit the criteria Gia had given him. The problem was she didn't have enough definitive information to narrow down his search enough. Ric had ended up with thousands upon thousands of results. Far too many to weed through.

"Don't worry," he said. "We'll figure something out. This isn't the end."

Although he had serious doubts if she was ever going to find her father. He knew what that frustration felt like. He knew she'd never truly give up hope. He still hadn't. Every now and then he would come across something that would spark a new search, and as usual, it would lead him down a rabbit hole that led nowhere.

He didn't want that for Gia. And then he had a thought.

"Do you have your mother's journal?" he asked as he led her to a nearby coffee shop.

"I do. Why?"

He held up a finger, signaling for her to wait.

By then they'd entered the nearly empty coffee shop, as most people were at work at that hour. They placed their order. He wanted to wait until they were seated at a table before he posed his proposal to her. The bistro was quick, and in no time they were holding one steaming espresso for him and a latte for her. They headed over to a table by the window.

"I can't wait any longer," she said. "What do you have in mind?"

"I wonder if you'd be willing to lend me your mother's journal. I have a friend who's good at locating people. I don't know why I didn't think of this sooner." Actually, he had. He knew Gia would resist the idea, but now that they were out of options, she might agree. "But if you were to allow my friend to read your mother's journal, he might be able to unearth some clues that were overlooked."

Gia was already shaking her head before he said the last words. "No. I couldn't do that. It's private."

"I can vouch that he's very discreet."

Gia continued to shake her head. "It wouldn't be right."

"So you're okay with giving up and never finding your father?" He knew the answer before he asked the question, but he doubted Gia had come to terms with what her decision would mean.

Gia finally stopped shaking her head. She stared at him, and he could see in her eyes that she was turning over the idea and weighing her options. "Your friend, he doesn't need the original, does he?"

Ric noticed the hesitant look on her face. It was though there was an internal struggle waging within her. "I don't know."

"I couldn't do that. I couldn't lend someone my mother's last words. I… I couldn't."

"I understand. I'll talk to him. Maybe we can scan the book or make photocopies. Would you be all right with that?"

She stirred her coffee. "I guess so."

That was all the affirmation he needed. He reached for his phone and signaled that he'd be right back. He wanted to make the arrangements before she changed her mind.

He knew if she didn't do absolutely everything within her power to locate her father, she would regret it. Maybe not today. Maybe not tomorrow. But one day she would look back on this moment, wondering why she didn't have the courage to do whatever it took. And Ric didn't want her to have any regrets—not about this.

After a brief phone conversation and promising access to his yacht for a future unnamed date, his friend said he'd look at it. But Nate made it known there were no guarantees. In his line of work, sometimes things worked out and sometimes he would hit a dead end. Ric told him he understood, but Nate wasn't referring to him but rather Gia. She shouldn't get her hopes up, but he would do his best.

"Well, what did he say?" she asked as soon as Ric returned to the table.

"He can't guarantee results, but he'll take the case."

"I understand." Then the worry returned to her face. "And the journal. Does he need the original?"

Ric shook his head. "He said we can scan the pages and send them to him."

Gia visibly exhaled. "Okay. I can do this." And then for the first time since they'd left the courthouse, a smile came over her face. "I have hope again. And it's all thanks to you. I wish there was some way I could pay you back."

"Don't worry about it."

"But I do. You've gone above and beyond for me. I will pay you back."

He knew she meant it, but it wasn't necessary. "I just want you to have a happy ending."

Not everyone got those, but Gia had a big heart for stray puppies and stray CEOs. She deserved her happy ending, and he'd do whatever he could to make sure she got it.

He told himself that it wasn't anything more

than he'd do for a friend. Because that's all they were—friends. He couldn't let it be more—even though it was tempting.

In the end, she'd be gone. And he'd once more be alone. He couldn't risk losing someone else he cared about. It was best to keep his beautiful houseguest at arm's length.

CHAPTER EIGHT

A DEAD END.

That was the opposite of what she'd been hoping for.

The next morning, Gia squinted at the bright sunlight streaming through her bedroom window. She yawned and stretched. She had zero motivation to get out of bed. Her lack of sleep might have something to do with it.

After staring into the dark, she'd turned on her light and combed through her mother's journal again, searching for any clue to the identity of her father. If she couldn't find anything, how was Ric's friend going to turn up anything? Still, when they'd returned from the café yesterday, Ric had helped her painstakingly scan the journal and email it to his friend.

Gia had all her hopes and dreams pinned on Ric's friend working miracles. After all she'd been through, her journey just couldn't end like this. There had to be a clue.

By the time she'd showered and spent a little more time than normal applying her makeup, she found Ric sitting out on the terrace, drinking his morning coffee. Well, not so much drinking as holding his coffee while staring blindly off into the clear blue sky. It seemed she wasn't the only one that day with something on their mind.

And she felt guilty. She'd taken up a lot of his time and kept him away from his office. He needed to know that he didn't need to stay here and babysit her. She and the pup would be just fine on their own.

Speaking of Gin, she hadn't seen the little guy all morning. In fact, she hadn't seen him since she'd finally slipped off into a restless sleep last night. As she stepped out onto the terrace, she was surprised to find him lying at Ric's feet. Those two had certainly bonded. Immediately the puppy spotted her and ran over for some cuddle time. She bent over to pick him up.

"I'm sorry."

Ric turned to her. "For what?"

"I fell asleep last night and didn't notice that Gin had wandered off. I hope he wasn't too much bother."

Ric didn't say anything for a moment. "He was fine once I got him out of my shoe closet. He seems to think my leather dress shoes are good chew toys."

"Oh, no!" Gia pressed a hand to her chest. "I'm so sorry. Let me know how much they were and I'll pay for them."

Ric shook his head. "No need. It was my fault for leaving the door open."

Gia frowned at Gin. "Naughty puppy. You have to be a good boy or Ric will toss us to the curb."

When Gin started to wiggle, she put him down. Gia had an idea she wanted to run past Ric, but first, she needed caffeine.

In the kitchen she poured herself a cup of coffee, leaving barely enough room for sweetener and creamer. A swish of the spoon and then she eagerly lifted it to her lips. She drank in the steamy brew and moaned her glee.

With cup in hand, she returned to the terrace. Gin was hot on her heels. Ric was still sitting there, once again staring into space. Whatever he was thinking about definitely had a hundred percent of his attention.

"Mind if I join you?" she asked softly, so as not to startle him.

He lowered his cup to the small table and turned to her. He smiled, but it didn't quite reach his eyes. "Please do."

Gin ran up to him and put his paws on his leg. The pup excitedly barked at Ric. The little guy was doing so well that they'd dispensed with his plastic cone.

Ric laughed and picked up the little dog, settling him on his lap. While those two went through their morning ritual, Gia made herself comfortable in the other chair. All the while, she tried to figure out what to say.

She raised her gaze to find Gin giving Ric a kiss. "I'd like to pay for the investigation. Whatever it is, just let me know."

Ric shook his head. "That won't be necessary."

"But I insist."

"There's nothing to pay. My friend, Nate, and I have a mutually beneficial arrangement, so he's doing it pro bono."

"Oh." Still, she just couldn't take any more charity from this man. She had been raised to carry her own weight. "Then let me pay you."

Ric again shook his head. "That won't be necessary."

He was not making this easy for her. "I appreciate everything you've done for me, but there has to be something I can do for you in return."

"You're serious, aren't you?"

"I am. My parents raised me to be independent and not to rely on the generosity of others." And then the thought about his uncle's villa came back to her. She still wasn't sure how Ric would feel about it, but it was worth mentioning.

JENNIFER FAYE 109

"I could work on cleaning up your uncle's place, you know, so it's ready for you to sell."

Ric arched a brow as he studied her. "And you feel you're up to the challenge?"

She nodded. "I did a good job with my hotel. I can show you pictures."

"Actually, I've seen the pictures online. Your hotel is beautiful. But my uncle's house would need a whole lot of updates to come close to looking that good. Surely you can't do it by yourself."

"Oh. Sorry. I didn't mean to imply I would. I'll work on the design, with your approval of course, and then I'll hire contractors or we can do it together, if you desire."

Ric's lips pressed together as though he were mulling it over. "And how long do you think it will take?"

"If the contractors are available, I wouldn't think too terribly long." And then a thought came to her. "You aren't planning on tearing down walls or anything drastic, are you?"

"The walls stay. The kitchen and bathrooms need to be gutted."

"I agree."

"But will you be around that long?" His gaze searched hers.

"Probably not. When we find my father, I'll want to spend time with him." When Ric frowned, she added, "But if we get started right away, the design should be in place. You'll be able to oversee the finishing touches. And then you won't have to worry about it sitting around being neglected."

He was quiet for a moment. "I like the idea. I'll make sure you have whatever funds you need. You know you really don't have to do this."

"But I want to do it." She truly did. It would be a much welcome distraction from the search for her father. "I went to design school, but with my parents passing, I never really got to put my education to use, aside from internships and working on the hotel."

"If you're an interior designer, why are you running a hotel?" He looked genuinely confused.

She shrugged. "It just worked out that way." But that answer didn't seem to appease him. And so she decided to tell him about her parents' very unusual will. "When my parents died, they left the estate to the sibling who could generate the biggest profit with the villa and vineyard."

"But what about the other two siblings?"

"They'll inherit an equal fortune."

"Do you want the estate?"

She shrugged. "I did at first, but now, I don't know."

"Why would you change your mind?"

"Because now I know I'm not a Bartolini. Not by blood. It seems the estate should go to a true

Bartolini." It made her sad to admit it. She felt different now. She couldn't explain it to anyone, but until she found her father, she'd never truly know who she was.

Sympathy showed in Ric's eyes. "But you were raised a Bartolini. If your parents didn't feel you were a Bartolini, don't you think they'd have told you?"

Gia shrugged. "It doesn't change the fact that I need to find my biological father. Once I find him, I'll be able to figure out what comes next."

"And if you don't find him?"

His pointed questions poked and prodded her, making her consider things she'd put off until now. "I can't think about it because…because it would mean I'll never know the answers to my past. I just know that if I can find my father that…that…"

"That you won't feel so alone anymore? That it will lessen the pain of losing both of your parents?"

How dare he say those things to her? She jumped to her feet. "You don't know what you're saying. You don't understand."

And with that, she turned and forced herself to walk in slow steady steps with her spine straight and her head held high. Gin trailed behind her. She wouldn't let Ric see how deeply his words had hurt her.

Had they hurt her? Or was it just that he was right? No. She wasn't trying to find a replacement for her parents. She would never do that.

All she wanted were answers, and there was nothing wrong with that. She needed to know about the part of her life that was missing. Who was her father? Had he known about her? And where did they go from here?

He'd utterly mucked that up.

Royally.

The next day, Ric was still worried about Gia. She was getting her hopes up for a happy reunion with her biological father, and Ric was worried that might not happen. Sure, his PI friend was good but sometimes good wasn't enough. His friend had searched for Ric's own father and come up with nothing. Absolutely nothing.

Maybe his mother had been right. Maybe it really had been a bad time in her life and she'd lost control. Ric didn't understand losing control like that because he always made sure he was in charge of everything from his business to his personal life. He had definite plans for both— none of which included a beautiful woman or a stray dog.

Speaking of the pup, no one had claimed Gin. It was looking more and more like the little guy was permanently theirs—correction, Gia's.

Mrs. Rossi had offered to take Gin for a walk to the park after the little guy was caught ripping a pair of Ric's socks to shreds. Why exactly had he said the dog could stay? The recollection was becoming fuzzier with each item of Ric's that the puppy turned into some sort of chew toy. He reminded himself that soon they'd be gone, and he'd resume his quiet existence. However, that idea didn't sound as appealing as it once had.

Not wanting to examine his feelings for Gia, he turned his thoughts to getting the reclusive owner of Grosso Global Transports to sit down with him for a meeting. Ric knew if he were to publicly announce what his program did that bids would come pouring in. But a bidding war wasn't what he had in mind. Money wasn't his goal with this project.

He wanted to test his technology with the biggest global transport company. If he could master their system, he could take what he'd done and duplicate it into something to help those in need. It would be a supply corridor using the goodwill of commercial transporters. That was his ultimate goal, but for companies to sign on to the emerging plan, he had to show them that he knew what he was doing and could make it work.

Tap. Tap.

Ric glanced up to find Gia standing in the doorway of his study. The sadness in her eyes

wanted more than
ness with a smile,
l her father for her.
he asked.

meaning to speak
ou wanted to hear

ave gotten so de-

ch a pessimist."
st—something I'm
t down in the chair
wrung her hands,
upset. "I just need
horrible happening
e of it."

. And just because
or him didn't mean

you changed your
e villa?"
m she was giving
with her was best
e out of his mouth
en't."

for?

ive smile lifted the
n't reach her eyes.
e you're busy."

He didn't want her to leave. He told himself it was because he wanted to cheer her up, but deep down he knew he craved her companionship for more selfish reasons—reasons he wasn't ready to acknowledge.

When he glanced up, she was already at the doorway. "Wait. I need your help."

He didn't have a clue what he needed her help with, but this wasn't the first time he'd been stuck in a position where he had to think on his feet.

She immediately turned back. "You do?"

Was that a flicker of interest in her eyes? Or was he only seeing what he wanted to see? It didn't matter; he'd started down this path and now he had to keep going.

He glanced down at his desk, and the only things on it were related to his current project. "Yes, I do." He had to go with what he had, though he wasn't sure how she would be able to help him. "I'm having a problem getting a reclusive businessman to meet with me. And it's really important." As he spoke, she ventured back into the office. "Everyone in the business knows he only signs on with the best of the best."

"So his working agreement is like the gold standard?"

"Exactly." He smiled, hoping she'd do the same. She didn't. But that didn't stop him from trying. "And I just have to get him to buy my technology."

Instead of smiling, she frowned. "Is this the meeting I interrupted on that first day at your uncle's villa."

"Yes. Well, no, you had nothing to do with it being canceled. I just need to figure out a way to lure him to a face-to-face meeting. I know if we can meet, I can convince him to buy into my technology."

"So what's the problem?"

"He's claiming there's no proof my program works."

"Didn't you test it?"

"Of course I did." The words rushed out of his mouth with a rumble of frustration. When Gia's eyes widened, he realized his error. In a friendlier tone, he said, "But it was in a closed system with a simulated world."

"So you need something in the real world?"

He nodded before rubbing the stiff muscles in his neck. His head started to throb.

"You seem like a man who knows everyone. Just pick someone out and try your program on their business."

"If only it were that easy, but I don't have anyone I trust in that line of business. And I can't afford for news of my development to get out into the public. I can't have another company steal the concept before I have a chance to use it to help others."

"Help others?"

He nodded again. And then he told her about his quest to provide an efficient and free mode of transportation for goods to those in need. It was when he finished his pitch that she smiled. Not a little smile but a big beautiful smile that lit up her eyes.

"That's an amazing endeavor. And it's so big. I mean, it would provide a transportation route to anywhere in the world. And people who never considered donating goods could do so without any real cost to them."

He nodded. "And the best part is that it wouldn't cost the transportation companies much money because my program would streamline everything, and no one company would take on the burden of delivering all of the packages. It would be a shared effort. But those companies, both big and small, would have to trust me with their vital information—the backbone of their business. To gain their trust would take something major."

"Hence the need to convince Mr. Grosso to buy your technology."

"Exactly."

"What exactly does your program do?" Genuine interest was written all over her beautiful face.

He normally didn't tell people about his work, most especially the things that were still being developed or that hadn't been sold yet, but Gia wasn't just anyone. He wanted to share this with her. Her stamp of approval meant a lot to him.

"You have to promise not to share any of this with anyone. In my world, it's all about who comes up with the idea first."

"Don't worry. I won't tell a soul. Your secret is safe with me because honestly, I'm lucky I know how to turn on a computer and enter reservation information. But that doesn't mean I don't want to hear about your work."

That was all the encouragement he needed. He started talking, laying out the generalities of what his algorithm could do for the transportation industry and how it could help charitable causes.

"That's amazing. And you did all of that by yourself?"

He nodded. He wasn't used to people praising him.

"You're a genius. But don't you have a company to run?"

He nodded again. "I quickly grow bored with paperwork. I need to keep myself in touch with technology, and I start my own personal projects. Sometimes they don't work out, and other times they explode into something bigger than I ever imagined." Not wanting the whole conversation to revolve around him, he said, "I'm sure that's how you felt when you started your own hotel."

She shrugged. "Not exactly."

"But you must have been excited to take on such a big venture."

"I like dealing with people. They are the best part of the business. And I had a lot of fun turning the villa into a boutique hotel. But I didn't go into the venture because it was a dream of mine."

"What is your dream?"

She shook her head. "It doesn't matter."

"Sure, it matters. Life is short. You need to be passionate about the time you spend on this earth."

She arched a brow. "I didn't figure you for a philosopher."

"It's something my uncle used to tell me. At the time, I didn't think he was serious. I thought he was just trying to get me to go do things and leave him alone."

"But now you know different?"

Ric nodded. "He was trying to help me, but I was too young and too angry with my mother to notice."

"But you remembered and that counts. And you listened to him. Because if anyone is passionate about their work, it's you."

He smiled. She was right. He hadn't thought of it that way, but in a sense, he'd honored his uncle's memory. He just wished his uncle was here so he could tell him thank you for always being there for him—even when he wasn't the easiest to deal with. And…and that he loved him. He was the father that he'd never had.

"Thanks," he said. When Gia sent him a puzzled look, he added, "For helping me realize that my uncle cared."

"I didn't do anything. You would have stumbled over those papers eventually."

"Would I have? I don't know. I was so determined that he didn't care to the point I might have thrown all that stuff out without paying much attention. But you made sure that didn't happen. So thank you."

"You're welcome, though I still don't think I did much."

He glanced down at his desk. "It seems we got off topic."

"Oh, yes. You need to figure out how to show Mr. Grosso that your program works in the real world but without telling anyone." She frowned as though giving it some serious consideration. "I'm not sure you can do that unless you were to try it on my business. But I don't transport anything."

Ric shook his head, dismissing the idea.

"Which is a shame because now that my sister has pulled out of the wedding business to marry the prince of Patazonia, the business at the hotel is spiraling."

"Wait. Your sister is marrying a prince?" When she nodded, he asked, "How is it that we've been sharing this apartment and puppy all of this time and you've failed to share this most interesting bit of your life?"

Gia laughed. "Like you're interested in fairy tales."

"I am when they concern you. So your sister… she's really going to become a princess?"

Gia nodded. "The royal wedding is set for Christmas."

"Next year."

Gia shook her head. "This year. The prince is going to be crowned king on New Year's."

"Wow. Your sister isn't just going to be a princess but a queen. And you're good with all of this?"

"Why wouldn't I be? I love my sister and want her to be happy."

"But you haven't found your father."

"One thing doesn't have anything to do with the other."

Ric nodded in understanding. "So your hotel, it isn't doing well because your sister isn't offering wedding packages?"

"Actually, her assistant, Sylvie, has taken over the wedding business. My sister still oversees it but mostly from a distance. Apparently, there's a lot to do before a royal wedding."

Ric was concerned for Gia. If she didn't find her biological father, she was going to need the hotel to focus on, and the last thing she'd need was to deal with a failing business. There had to be a way of turning things around.

He had to give it some thought. His algorithm was geared toward a lot larger, complex system. Still, there were components of it that dealt with bringing in business from individuals as well as other businesses. Would it be possible to rework the algorithm to scale it down to bringing in customers to a hotel? It was a stretch. A big stretch. But he was up for the challenge.

CHAPTER NINE

THINGS WERE LOOKING UP.

At least where the villa was concerned. The search for Gia's father was still a wait and see scenario.

More than a week had passed since Ric had agreed to let Gia work on his uncle's villa. She hadn't wasted one single moment. It felt so good to be productive. Sitting around just wasn't for her.

Ric had spent a lot of time in his study. Gia wasn't sure how much time he spent at his office, as she had the go-ahead to hire a construction crew and to start work on his uncle's villa. Not just a couple of men but a whole army of them, tackling different rooms at once. Ric wanted this job done as quickly as possible, and he was willing to pay whatever it cost.

Gia was so excited about taking this run-down home and turning it into something magical that the wait for news about locating her biological father wasn't nearly as excruciating. She'd even started taking calls from her siblings, who were so relieved to speak directly to her instead of getting by with sporadic text messages.

And Gin went with her every day to the villa. Though the pup was interested in making it to the garden in back, Gia was having none of it. He was hurt back there once; they weren't having a repeat episode. Though the garden was on her list of things to do, it had moved down in the order of priority because the gardener couldn't fit her in for a couple of weeks.

Gia wasn't one to bark out orders and stand back; she was the type who liked to get her hands dirty. She blamed it on her— She paused. She blamed it on Aldo. Even though they weren't biologically connected, she couldn't ignore how much they had in common. Aldo had enjoyed getting his hands dirty at the vineyard, testing the soil, sampling the grapes and fixing the irrigation system.

And so she'd spent the day patching walls and prepping them for fresh paint. In all honesty, the villa's bones were in awesome shape. And with Ric wanting to keep the layout as it was, this job was going to go quickly. It was more a touch-up than a remodel. Still, she enjoyed it. The villa had a rich history and warmth to it that drew her in.

There was a marble floor in the spacious

foyer, with a crystal chandelier. Both were staying. They just needed to be cleaned until they gleamed. Each room had tall windows, and when the old drapes were removed, the Mediterranean sun lit up the place. What wasn't there to like?

The walls had ornate trim that was unique but not over-the-top. Gia made sure to tell the crew it was to remain. Any trim that was damaged by a leak in the roof was to be repaired or if worse came to worst, it was to be re-created. She knew plasterwork could be a painstaking job, but it added so much character to the house. It was like this villa had its own personality. Some family was going to be very lucky to live there.

She thought of Ric living in the villa. It was a lot of house for one person to live in alone. But would he always be alone? She could easily imagine him with a baby in his arms. The child would be laughing because Ric had just tickled them. Gia found herself smiling at the image.

Then a beautiful woman entered Gia's image. The woman was tall, slender and gorgeous. She was smiling as she came to lean into Ric. They both fussed over the child. She would be his wife.

Gia blinked away the troubling image. It was best she focused on the here and now. And right now, she had to hurry and get to the villa. The kitchen floor had been put in, and the cabinets were being delivered today.

She glanced in the mirror, taking in her newly bought navy-blue T-shirt, which hugged her curves, and the new jeans with the perfectly placed worn holes near the front pockets and her hips. She smiled. If her mother knew how much she'd paid for jeans that already had holes in them, she would lecture her about wasting her money. As her mother's voice filled her mind, Gia's smile broadened.

She missed her mother. She may be mad at her for keeping such an important part of her life from her, but she really missed her. She missed being able to talk to her as they cooked in the kitchen together.

Gia wanted to tell her mother about Gin and his boundless energy. But more importantly, she wanted to tell her about Ric and how amazing she found him. She knew her mother would take things out of context and suggest she date Ric. At which point she would tell her mother she couldn't. He was a workaholic and she, well, she was still figuring herself out. It was bad timing among other reasons…

Tap. Tap.

"Yes?" Gia called out.

The door opened, and Gin barked before running over to Ric. He smiled and bent to pet the puppy. It gave Gia a moment to study him. Wasn't that the same shirt he'd had on the night before?

And his hair, it was unusually scattered. What was up with that?

When Ric straightened, there were shadows beneath his eyes. "I was wondering if you had a couple of minutes to talk."

That sounded serious. "Should I be worried?"

He shook his head. "Nothing for you to worry about. I just have a proposal for you."

Proposal? Suddenly her thoughts went in the wrong direction. Flowers. Candlelight. Ric down on one knee—

She screeched her thoughts to a halt. Where in the world had that come from? She wasn't ready to settle down. Not with Ric. Not with anyone.

She swallowed hard, trying to calm her nervousness. "A proposal?"

He nodded. "It'd be easier if we did this in my study."

Without waiting for her response, he turned to walk away. Gin was hot on his heels. Gia stood there for a moment, wondering what was up with him. And then curiosity had her following.

When she reached his study, she came to a complete halt. Her gaze took in the scene before her. Ric's usually clean study, where everything was in its place, was in complete disarray. There were papers scattered across the desktop with his oversize monitor and keyboard in the center. There were coffee mugs, not just one or two but many of them here and there. Empty dinner dishes were stacked on an end table. And the curtains were drawn. There was no indication that it was a beautiful sunny day outside.

"What in the world happened in here?" Gia moved to the windows and drew back the heavy curtains to let the sunshine stream in. It didn't help the state of the office. "Have you been living in here?"

"Sort of."

"Aren't those the same clothes you had on yesterday?"

He glanced down and then ran a hand over the wrinkled shirt as though it might actually improve his appearance in some small way. "They might be."

She arched a brow. "Might be?"

"Okay. They are." He sat down behind the desk in a red-and-white gaming chair. "But you have to understand, this is the way I get when I'm involved in a project."

"So nothing is wrong?"

He shook his head. "For once, I think something is right."

Her heart seemed to pause. She'd been working so hard to keep herself distracted, but with each day that passed, she grew more anxious.

"Is it my biological father? Is there news?"

Ric shook his head. "I'm sorry for being so

cryptic. There's no news yet, but don't give up hope. These things take time."

Her heart sunk down to her new work boots. She didn't want Ric to see how disappointed she was, so she sucked down her disappointment. "What's had you so preoccupied?"

"That's what I wanted to talk to you about. I've been working on modifications and scaling down the program. It's taken a lot of work, but I think it was worth it—"

"Whoa! Slow down. You lost me."

He visibly drew in a breath and blew it out. "Sorry. I think I need some sleep. You gave me the idea the other day when we were talking. And I thought we could help each other. My program needs a practical application and your hotel business needs people directed to it, so I've been working to marry the two."

"You have?" She hadn't been expecting this. She sank down on the armchair near his desk.

"Well, not exactly. I've been working on modifications to my program to see if it was even possible. And now I think it is. I need your permission so I can access your hotel files."

"Wait. But I thought your program was to streamline transportation of goods?"

"It is. But I modified it so that instead of goods, it's moving people to your hotel. So it will access public transportation, airlines, boats, whatever to make the trip to your hotel expedient and economical."

"I... I don't know what to say."

"Say yes. I think it can help both of us." He paused. His gaze searching hers. "Will you let me access your system?"

"I... I don't know." She seemed to be saying that a lot lately. "What are you going to do?"

"I'm going to fine-tune things. I'll guarantee that your business won't decline when I'm done."

"You can't promise something like that."

He sent her a self-assured smile. "Sure, I can. Trust me."

She wanted to trust him. It'd be so easy to trust him. But she had the feeling they were talking about totally different things. While he wanted her to trust him with her business, she was daydreaming about something a lot more personal.

How could she turn him down when he was pleading with his eyes? He wanted this. He needed this to prove that his program worked in the real world. And her hotel really needed more business now that her sister—the almost-princess of Patazonia—was no longer running the wedding portion of the business.

"Okay. But on one condition—make that two conditions."

"Which would be?"

"You take a shower and get some sleep. And I want to be a part of this. I want to know what you're changing."

He frowned at her. "That's three conditions."

She thought about it. "So it is. What do you say?"

"Sleep is overrated."

She pressed her hands to her hips. "But showers aren't."

"Point taken. And I suppose a nap wouldn't hurt. Coffee only goes so far."

"Good. We can start when I get back. We're starting to put the kitchen together." She checked the time. "And I'm late. Get some rest."

"Yes, ma'am." He sent her a tired smile.

"I knew there was something I liked about you—you listen to me. Unlike someone else." Her gaze moved to the puppy. "Come, Gin."

The puppy didn't move from Ric's side.

"Gin." She tried again to get the puppy to come to her, but she was having no luck. She definitely saw some puppy obedience classes in Gin's future.

"Don't worry," Ric said. "He can stay with me."

"Are you sure? He might keep you awake."

"Between you and me, I'm so tired right now that I don't think anything could wake me once I'm out." His gaze moved to the puppy. He ran his hand over the pup's back. "And he's a good snuggler."

"Aw… I was wondering where he snuck off to at night."

"He climbs in my bed and steals a pillow."

She smiled. So Mr. Independent, Mr. I-Don't-Need-Anyone was hooked on the puppy. "Okay. You two be good. I've got to go."

And out the door she went, anxious to see the beginning of her vision for the villa's kitchen. But as excited as she was about the remodel, she couldn't help thinking of Ric. Every day she saw a little more of the man behind the CEO persona, and she was drawn in a little more.

She told herself not to get attached because soon she'd be leaving.

But what would it hurt to enjoy the time she had left here in Lapri? And to enjoy the time she spent with Ric as they worked on marrying his program with her business?

This wasn't good.

He couldn't concentrate.

Ric told himself that his inability to focus was because he hadn't taken a long enough nap like Gia had insisted upon. But the truth was, he was distracted by her closeness as they huddled around his computer.

She'd showered as soon as she'd returned from

the villa. And now, as she leaned in close to read something on the screen, he inhaled the gentle floral scent of her perfume. Her short hair was still damp, and she hadn't slowed down to put on any makeup. Even without primping, she was the most beautiful woman that he'd ever seen. In fact, he preferred the natural look on her.

He'd caught himself more than once staring at her and thinking he wanted nothing more than to pull her into his arms and kiss her. Thankfully, she hadn't seemed to notice he was distracted or that he'd hit the wrong key repeatedly, which wasn't like him at all.

He told himself to think of her as a client he was working with on a way to help her boutique hotel. And it worked for a little, but then she'd tucked a strand of hair behind her ear and now he was thinking about combing his fingers through the short, silky strands that accentuated her heart-shaped face.

His fingers paused on the keyboard, having lost his train of thought. "What's your password?"

"Sunflower01."

"That's it? No special characters?"

She shook her head. "I only added the numbers because the system insisted on it."

Concern filled him. "Do you know how easily hackers could crack such a simple password?"

She shrugged. "Who would want to break into our reservations system?"

"It's more than reserving rooms. There's payments and identities."

Gia frowned. "Okay. I get it. I have to be more careful."

Together they came up with a more elaborate password. And then she phoned Michael to inform him about the changes.

"And you need to set up a three-factor authentication," he said.

"Now you're being over the top with security."

"Actually, I'm not. Hackers are good. Very good. They just haven't found you yet, but when they do find your site, you'll have big problems. It could ruin the hotel's reputation."

"Are you serious?" When he nodded, she added, "Hackers really need to get a life instead of making everyone else's so difficult."

They went about setting up the three-factor authentication. He could tell Gia wasn't happy about all of the extra steps, but he assured her that in the end, she would appreciate her business being secure. She merely nodded and continued to frown. He couldn't help but smile. The little frown lines between her brows were adorable.

And he knew the more adorable she became, the more hooked on her he became. That was dangerous. Once her biological father was located, she'd be gone. He'd once more be alone.

The evening flew by.

Gia did her best to walk Ric through her online system, but she didn't always know what he was asking. It seemed he knew more about the program without having to work on it than she did after using it for months. But then again, computer programs were his thing, not hers.

She ordered a pizza and insisted Ric take a break to eat. She even persuaded him to join her on the couch with Gin taking his usual spot between them, waiting for a scrap of food to fall so he could scarf it up.

"You know, you don't have to go to all of the extra trouble with my website," Gia said, feeling guilty that he was spending time fixing her security and search engine optimization.

"I don't mind. In fact, I enjoy this type of work."

"Have you always been good at computers?" She'd seen another side of him while they'd been working on her website—a side that was nothing like the man in the movie or the headlines posted about him on the internet. A wickedly smart, funny and caring man—a man any woman would be foolish not to fall for.

He finished his last bite of pizza, wiped his

mouth and then set aside the empty plate. "I started messing around with computers when my uncle gave me one for my eighth birthday."

"Your uncle? Not your mother?"

He was quiet for a moment. "My mother wasn't in my life much as a kid."

"Oh, I'm sorry. I didn't know."

"Nobody knows because I don't talk about it."

"I shouldn't have said anything. Sometimes my mouth gets ahead of me."

"It's okay. It'd be natural to assume I'd have grown up with my mother, but she wasn't the maternal kind most people have. I'm sure your mother baked you cookies, helped with your homework and tucked you in at night."

It was true. She'd always thought she'd had the best mother in the entire world. And then she and her siblings had read their mother's journal. Those cherished memories grew tarnished. Sometimes she wished they'd just burned her journal and let the fire consume her mother's secret. And other times, she was excited about the future and meeting this mystery man who was her biological father.

"But you have to remember," Gia said, "my mother lied to me my entire life. So she wasn't perfect."

Ric reached out and took her hand in his. He

gave it a squeeze. "No one is perfect. But your mother loved you."

"I'm sure your mother loves you too."

He shook his head. "I was always a bother—a mistake."

This time Gia squeezed his hand and leaned her head against his shoulder. "I'm sorry. Looks like both of our mothers let us down."

"I guess."

"At least you had your uncle. Was he always there for you?"

"He was. I took his quietness for aloofness, but thanks to you finding all those papers he'd saved from my youth, I realize that I misjudged him. And for that I'm really sorry. I remember one time he threw me a surprise birthday party. It wasn't really my thing, but he made sure all of my classmates were there—"

As Ric regaled her with stories of his childhood, she felt the walls between them coming down. Beneath his cool, business exterior there was a really warm, passionate man. And she was utterly falling for him—falling for his deep soothing voice; falling for the gentle rumble of his laugh; falling for *him*.

"I really should get back to work," Ric said.

That was her cue to release his hand even though it felt so natural to have his fingers laced with hers. And it was time to sit upright, instead of letting her shoulder lean into his. It was with great reluctance that she did those things. Once they were no longer touching, she missed the warmth of his touch—the coziness they'd shared.

She turned to him to say how much this time had meant to her at the same moment he turned to her. Their faces were so close. If she were just to lean forward ever so slightly, her lips would press to his. And what would be the problem with that? After all they'd shared this evening, a kiss was the perfect way to end it. Or would it just be the beginning?

Without thinking of the consequences, Gia leaned forward. Her lips pressed to his. He didn't move at first, as though unsure what to do about this new situation. Gia was more than willing to show him what she had in mind.

He continued to sit perfectly still. Was he shocked by her actions? How was that possible? She was certain plenty of women had thrown themselves at him. Not that she was throwing herself at him.

She was—she thought for a moment—sampling him. Her lips moved over his smooth ones. Definitely sampling—like he was the finest, most decadent tiramisu dessert. And she loved desserts!

Then there was a groan—or was it a moan?

Had the sound come from him? Or her? But then it didn't matter because he'd reached out to her, stroking her cheek. He met her kiss for kiss. She was getting lost in the moment.

Why exactly had she waited all this time? Kissing Ric was something that should be done often—as in twice in the morning, at least three times at lunch and definitely all evening long.

His tongue touched her lips, seeking access. She opened herself up to him, anxious to take this to the next level. She couldn't get enough of him. He was so addictive.

As his tongue probed and stroked her, a moan swelled in the back of her throat. No kiss had ever been quite like this one—

Buzz. Buzz.

No. No. No. Just ignore it. It'll stop.

Not the kissing. Definitely not the kissing. She never wanted it to end. Apparently Ric felt the same way as he reached out and pulled her closer—her soft curves aligning with his hard planes. At some unknown point Gin had discreetly disappeared, leaving the couch all theirs. Mmm…

Buzz. Buzz.

It was Ric who pulled back. "You should get that. It might be important."

"Me? Isn't it your phone?"

They both reached for their phones on their

respective end tables. Ric was right. It was her phone. And it was the contractor.

"I'm sorry," she said. "It's work."

Ric nodded in understanding. While she pressed the phone to her ear, Ric returned to his desk and started running his fingers over the keyboard once more.

Upon answering the phone, she heard shouting in the background. She dispensed with pleasantries. "What's wrong?"

"We have a water leak in the kitchen," the contractor said.

"The kitchen?" She didn't even want to think of what the water would ruin. "I'll be right there." Once she ended the call, she looked at Ric. He was already absorbed in marrying his algorithm with her business's website. "I've got to run out."

"No problem. I'll be here when you get back."

Gia got to her feet. She couldn't leave quite yet. She stepped up to the desk. Not sure what to say or how to say it. Still, she had to know where they stood. His fingers stopped typing, and his gaze lifted to meet hers.

Her heart pounded in her chest. "About what happened—"

"Don't worry. We can talk about it later. Go deal with your problem."

"You're sure?" She felt weird kissing him one moment and running out the door the next.

JENNIFER FAYE   141

"Positive. We're good. Now go."

So she did as he said. But she couldn't help but wonder where it would have led them if they hadn't been interrupted. Was Ric falling for her too?

hadn't been interrupted. Was Ric falling for her

CHAPTER TEN

THINGS WERE DEFINITELY coming along.

The walls were painted.

The counters were in.

The floor was finished.

Three days later, Gia stood in the center of the
spacious kitchen and turned around. They still
had a lot of details to work on, like the back-
splash, the fixtures and the cabinet pulls. Things
that would make this house a home. Lucky for
them, the leaking pipe had been caught before it
caused any major damage.

A smiled lifted her lips. This place had an old-
world feel but with all the modern conveniences.
Though the long center island did give the room
a more modern vibe, she'd weighed need over
authenticity. But they'd made sure the island
matched the look and feel of the cabinetry. All in
all, anyone would be lucky to have this kitchen.
She'd certainly feel that way if it were hers.

She couldn't help but wonder if Ric would

change his mind about the place and move in once it was completed. After all, he'd grown up here. It was a part of his past—

"There you are." The sound of Ric's voice came from behind her.

She turned to him. "You were looking for me?"

"I've been calling you and texting you. Didn't you get my messages?"

"Sorry. My phone is in the other room." She couldn't help but worry that something was wrong. It wasn't usual for Ric to track her down in person. "Is something wrong with Gin?"

"No." He shook his head. "He's fine. He's at home with Mrs. Rossi."

"Then what's wrong?"

"Nothing is wrong. Not exactly."

"You aren't making any sense." And her anxiety was climbing with each passing moment.

"It's about your father—your biological father. Nate called—"

"He figured it out?" Excitement flooded her veins. "He knows the man's name?"

"No. I'm sorry. He wasn't able to uncover any additional information from the pages we scanned to him. But he has an idea that might lead to more information about him. However, it's going to take your agreement."

"What is it?" She was getting desperate. She

couldn't stop now. She felt as though they were very close to finding out his name.

"Nate needs the actual journal to run some tests on. He might need to remove a page or two."

For the briefest moment, Gia hesitated. She worried her bottom lip. It was her mother's final words. If anything happened to it, she'd be miserable. But her siblings had given their blessings for her to do with the journal what was necessary to locate her biological father. Maybe the risk was worth it.

"Okay. Do it," she said in a rushed breath before she could take it back.

Ric arched a brow. "I know how protective you are of your mother's journal. Are you sure? I don't know exactly what he's going to do with it."

"I'm sure." She wasn't. Not really. But her mother used to say, nothing ventured, nothing gained. "It's back at your place."

"Can you leave now? Nate has some time this afternoon."

"I...uh, yes. Just let me have a word with the contractor."

"I'll meet you at the car."

"Sounds like a plan."

Gia thought of the scratched-out lines in her mother's journal. She'd always wondered if her mother regretted what she'd written. Or had she been afraid that someone else would read it?

Either way, this was it. She was certain they were going to get some answers now.

No matter the results…

Everything was about to change.

Ric wanted Gia to find her biological father and learn the answers to all her questions. And yet there was another part of him that didn't want her journey to end—not yet.

He was just getting used to sharing his apartment with her. And then there was the puppy. Who'd have thought he was a dog person, but he was. If it hadn't been for Gia, he'd have never figured that out.

He'd also learned that he enjoyed having someone to share morning coffee with. Not just anyone, Gia. She was talkative at all the right times. And when he just needed some companionable silence, she seemed to recognize that and leave him to his thoughts.

After stopping by the apartment for Gia to clean up and grab the journal, they headed off to the other side of the island. The trip was quiet as each was lost in their own thoughts.

What would happen when she learned the true identity of her father? She would leave. There would be no reason for her to stay. Sure, there was the villa to finish remodeling, but her plans were already written down. There was no reason someone else couldn't follow them. There would be no pressing reason for her to remain. And that thought dampened Ric's mood.

He parked at a research facility and followed his friend's instructions to the fifth floor where they were to meet Nate in the lobby. Ric checked the time. They were a few minutes early.

He told himself it would be good to get back to his solitary life. He could work as late as he liked. He could get up whenever he liked, but then again, he never slept in, no matter how late he worked. He wouldn't have to eat on a schedule. He could walk around his apartment in as little clothing as he liked—

"Are you sure Nate said to meet him here?" Gia's voice interrupted his thoughts.

"Um, yes, he did."

Just then Nate, a tall lanky man with sandy blond hair, rounded the corner. His gaze met Ric's. "Sorry to keep you waiting." He kept moving until he stopped in front of Gia. He held his hand out to her. "Gia, at last we meet. I'm Nate, and it's a pleasure to finally meet you in person."

"It's nice to meet you too." She flashed him a brilliant smile.

Was it Ric's imagination or did Nate hold Gia's hand longer than necessary? And the way he was smiling at her, it was like he was flirting with her.

Who could blame him? Gia was a knockout. But they were here to get some work done.

Ric cleared his throat and stepped closer. Gia pulled her hand back, but her face was flushed and she was still smiling. Why didn't she act like that around him?

"We should get to work," Ric said, wanting to move this along.

"Right. This way." Nate led them down a hallway and up a flight of steps. "I have a friend with a lab and some special equipment that should help us uncover what's crossed out in your mother's journal." Just outside the lab, Nate turned to her. "You do realize this might be a futile effort. This might not lead to any clues about your biological father."

"I understand." Gia had a certainty in her eyes. "But I have to do whatever is necessary."

"Even if it means removing the pages in question from the journal?"

Gia momentarily hesitated. "Even then."

Nate nodded in understanding. "Then let's do this."

Inside the lab, they shook hands with a shorter, older man. Gia was very quiet. Her hands tightly gripped the journal. And the smile had disappeared from her face.

"May I have the journal?" Nate asked.

Gia handed it over and then wrung her hands.

Nate quickly located a page with some crossed out writing. "I'm going to see if I can hold it up to a very bright light to see if we can make out the original writing."

They struggled to hold the journal up to the light. It quickly became evident that this process would work better if the page was removed from the journal. With a sharp knife, Nate sliced the page from the book near the spine.

And so they worked through a process starting with a bright light and then applying a blue light. Neither was able to distinguish the handwriting from the scratch-out marks.

Next, they tried applying some heat to warm the paper to see if it would make a difference with the ink. Again, it didn't work.

Finally they ran the page through a high-resolution scanner that was equipped with image editing software by applying a contrast. As the two men worked to get the contrast just right to display the text, Gia rubbed her rigid shoulders and clenched hands let Ric know her whole body was tense.

One look at her rigid shoulders and clenched hands let Ric know her whole body was tense. He wasn't sure how much more she was up for. She'd already endured so much when she lost her parents. This just had to work.

He moved close to her and draped his arm over her shoulders, drawing her to his side. He wasn't sure how she'd react, but the next thing he knew, she was leaning into him. He welcomed the warmth of her body. Her head landed against his shoulder. He leaned his head to the side, resting his cheek against her silky hair. He breathed in its floral scent from her shampoo.

He wasn't sure how long they stood there quietly waiting and watching. Gia didn't move. Neither did he. He wanted to be there for her—to be the pillar of strength she'd need if this experiment didn't yield the desired results.

"We got it!" Nate projected the image on the large monitor.

Gia let go of Ric as she rushed forward. "I can't believe it. It worked!"

"It did," Nate said. "It really helped that your mother used two different colored pens."

Ric moved to stand with them. His gaze focused on the words now revealed.

I'm so mad at Aldo. Why does he have to be such a jerk about the inheritance? His stupid pride. It always comes back to the money. I wish I'd never inherited it.

Ric wasn't exactly sure what that meant, but he was certain it was of no help in finding Gia's biological father. He turned his attention to her.

Her momentary excitement had deteriorated into a frown.

"I'm sorry it's not what you were hoping for," Ric said.

"Do it again." There was determination tinged with desperation in Gia's voice. "Whatever it costs, I'll pay it."

And so they did it again with another page.

And again, they uncovered her mother being upset with Aldo—for forcing a separation.

But it was on the third try that they uncovered something useful. Gia stood front and center, staring up at the screen.

Ric positioned himself behind her. His height enabled him to look over her to the words on the screen.

Stupid. Stupid. How could I have let this happen? Too much anger—too much wine— and a sweet-talking man. Now I'm pregnant with Berto Gallo's baby.

When I went to tell him, he never gave me a chance. He turned me away without letting me say a word. He said if I came back, he'd have me arrested. Arrested!

Oh, what a colossal mess.

The last words were blurred even with the high diagnostic equipment. It looked as if water had been spilled on the page, but just a couple of drops. Tears?

This man didn't sound like a good guy. Far from it. Ric felt really bad for Gia. He knew that she'd imagined a happy meeting with her biological father, and now it wasn't to be. He was ready to do anything to console her when she turned to him with a smile. A smile?

"This is it. We have his name." Her eyes shimmered with unshed tears. "Now I can track him down."

He couldn't tell if those were tears of sadness, relief or was it possibly she was truly happy about this discovery?

"Are you sure you still want to go through with—"

"Of course I am."

Ric opened his mouth, then, thinking better of it, he wordlessly closed it. At the very least, she was in shock. He couldn't let her continue on this journey alone.

He would be there to cheer with her if it worked out with her biological father. To dry her tears if it went awry. No matter what, she wasn't getting rid of him.

CHAPTER ELEVEN

ANY DAY NOW…

Any moment…

A couple of days had passed since the discovery of her father's name. Nate had promised to call when he had information about her father. Nothing. But soon.

She glanced over at Ric as he sat behind the wheel of his sporty coupe. "Ric, where are we going?"

A smile played the corners of his sexy mouth. "It's a surprise."

Hope bubbled up within her. "Did you find my father?"

The smile fell from his face. "Not yet. I'm sorry, Gia. I have people working on it." He reached out and took her hands in his. "It's a common name. And so far, he doesn't appear to be on the island. But we'll keep looking. But in the meantime, I have something to take your mind off the search."

He was so supportive and thoughtful. She wanted to smile—to be excited—but she was struggling. "What is it?"

"I can't tell you. Remember?"

"I know. It's a surprise."

"Right." There was a twinkle in his eyes, and she noticed that twinkle only appeared when he was up to something—something unexpected.

So what was he up to? She had no clues. All she knew was that it was a surprise. That's all he'd told her since that morning when he'd mentioned he had plans for them. He'd asked her to get all dressed up in her finest clothes.

It was a little black number because a black dress worked anywhere. It dipped low in the front, giving a hint of her cleavage and it left most of her back bare. She'd paired it with diamond earrings and a diamond pendant that her parents had given her on her twentieth birthday. For her feet, she'd selected a pair of silver-and-crystal-studded heals.

When she'd packed for the trip, she hadn't any idea what clothes would be needed once she met her father. She certainly hadn't expected to meet someone like Ric, so she was glad she'd had the foresight to pack an outfit like this. Life certainly worked in mysterious ways.

Gia glanced around as the city faded into the background.

Ric's luxurious midnight blue sports car glided over the roadway. He was in a particularly good mood. They'd both been working so hard that they hadn't been able to spend much time together. And when the evenings rolled around, they'd both collapse on the couch with Gin between them. Just like one big happy family.

Not that they were a family by any stretch of the imagination. Okay, maybe the thought crept into her imagination now and then. Was that so wrong? After all, once you got past Ric's prickly exterior, he was warm, thoughtful and fun. Any woman would be lucky to have him for a husband—

Not that she was thinking of him in that way. Suddenly the air grew warm. Gia's mouth grew dry as she chanced a quick glance in Ric's direction. His attention was focused on traffic instead of paying attention to her self-imposed discomfort. Thankfully.

The farther they got from downtown, the more she wondered what he was up to. "You do know that most of the restaurants are behind us?"

"Don't you trust me?"

"I do." The automatic admission surprised not only him, with his raised brows, but also herself. When did they change from being strangers to pleasant acquaintances to trusted friends? She didn't know, but she knew without a doubt that it was true. She trusted him.

"Good." He reached over and squeezed her hand. "I trust you too."

His response warmed a spot in her chest, but she refused to dwell on it. "Good. Now that we've established that, tell me where we're going."

"I can't."

She sighed. "Why not?"

"Because it'd ruin the surprise."

"What surprise? It's not my birthday." And then a thought came to her. "Is it your birthday?"

"No. And that's all I'm telling you."

She huffed and crossed her arms. She wanted to be mad at him but she couldn't. He was too sweet and thoughtful. He'd been spending every free moment to help her track down her father. He'd used his technology to help her hotel. And in turn, he'd given her a way to help pay him back by letting her help fix up his uncle's estate.

Her experience with remodeling her parents' villa and changing it into a boutique hotel had definitely come in handy. She'd learned so much the first time around, and she was learning more through this process. She was starting to wonder if the hotel business was really what she wanted to do with her life. She liked working with her hands, getting dirty and designing beautiful homes.

"Hey," Ric said, "you didn't have to go all quiet on me."

"Sorry. I was just thinking about your uncle's, or rather your, villa. It's come a long way. You should be able to put it on the market soon."

"The more you work on it, the harder it's going to be for me to part with it."

"Really?" She narrowed her gaze on him. "Or are you just saying that to make me feel good?"

He cast her a quick glance. "Would I do that?"

She didn't hesitate. "Yes, you would. You might fool other people with that occasional growl of yours, but not me. I've seen your soft side."

He laughed. "You have, huh?"

"I have. You're a softy."

He nodded. "I wonder if my assistant would agree with you."

"She would."

"You sound confident. Have you been discussing me with Marta?"

"Perhaps." She hadn't, but she'd let him wonder about that one.

"We're here."

She glanced around at the marina. This wasn't just any marina. The boats docked here weren't "just a boat." These beauties were big and expensive yachts. She'd never seen so many in the same spot.

She was confused. "What are we doing here?"

"Having dinner."

"Dinner? Here?"

He got out of the car without an answer, not that she was expecting one. She was still sitting there taking in the impressive view when her car door swung open. And there stood Ric in his black tux with a black tie and white shirt.

He held his hand out to Gia and helped her to her feet. As she placed her hand in his, his fingers wrapped around hers, sending a wave of energy up her arm. It set her heart pounding.

She told herself to calm down. This was probably another business dinner. No big deal. She would do her best to help him sell his technology. It was the least she could do after all he'd done to help her find her father.

As he guided her down to the docks, she asked, "Who are we meeting tonight? Is there anything I can say to help you?"

"Help me?"

"You know, to make a deal." She rambled on because she was nervous and he was still holding her hand, which was making thinking a challenge. "You can count on me to back you up. If you want me to tell them how your technology is helping my hotel, I can do that." Because ever since Ric had helped her strengthen her passwords, he'd also strengthened her hotel's online presence. Reservations were steadily climbing. "Just let me know what you want me to say."

A smiled played at the corners of his lips. "And that's what you think we're here for? Business?"

"Aren't we?" Her stomach shivered with nerves.

Ric stopped walking and turned to her. He gazed into her eyes. "No. We're here for something far more important."

She wanted to say something. But the pounding of her heart drowned out her thoughts. And instead she stood there quietly, as though by staring into his eyes he'd cast a spell over her. Her gaze momentarily lowered to his lips before she caught herself and raised her gaze to meet his once more.

He stepped closer to her and lowered his voice. "I wanted to do something special for you."

"You…you did?" She struggled to string two words together.

He smiled at her, and it was like a hundred butterflies took flight within her. He turned and they continued walking. What exactly had he planned for this evening? And what did it mean? Was this just a friendly gesture? Or was it something more?

When he came to a stop next to a huge white yacht with navy trim, her mouth gaped. They were going to board this? She'd never been on a boat before, let alone one so fancy.

Her family had money, but it was old money and her parents liked to live simply. Though they could have owned something like this beautiful vessel, they wouldn't have. The man she'd always thought of as her father hadn't liked the water, and her mother was happy with their life at the vineyard—at least that's what Gia and her siblings had thought until they'd uncovered their mother's journal and the circumstances surrounding Gia's conception.

She wondered what else they'd assumed about their parents and been wrong about. How could people be so close and yet not know as much about each other as they'd thought?

"Gia? What's wrong?" The concern in Ric's voice startled her from her troubling thoughts.

"Um, nothing."

The look on his face said that he didn't believe her. "Are you sure?"

"Positive." She forced a smile to her lips. "What are we doing here? I thought we were going out for dinner."

"We are." And then he led her aboard.

She looked around. The boat looked brand-new. Everything sparkled and gleamed. "How did you manage this?"

"It wasn't hard. The truth is that I don't use

it much. When I purchased the yacht, I thought I'd use it for business meetings and to entertain business acquaintances, but I quickly found out they were just as busy as me. No one these days has time for long, leisurely outings."

Her mouth gaped as she looked around again with the knowledge that this huge boat was all his. "This is bigger than the guest house on my parents' estate."

It wasn't until the words were out of her mouth that she realized the estate was no longer her parents'. It was still so hard to comprehend that they were gone, and now she was searching for where she fit in this world. What once was, was no longer.

"I should probably sell it, but I'm glad I didn't." He stepped up close to her.

"Why not?"

"Because then we wouldn't be able to have dinner out on the sea."

And with that the yacht pulled away from the dock, and they headed off into the sunset. Gia felt as though she were Cinderella, but this definitely wasn't a ball. It was better.

Once they were away from the shore, it was like they were the only ones on earth. Well, except for the staff that served them the most delightful dinner. And the captain who navigated the peaceful seas. However, they made themselves scarce, leaving her and Ric alone.

Ric had her full attention. He was sweet and attentive. She'd noticed that he hadn't checked his phone once since they'd left the dock. His attention was fully on her. And she had no idea what that meant. Was this the beginning of something? A follow-up to that steamy kiss they'd shared? Her heart quickened at the thought.

Thoughts of her business, the villa remodel and the search for her biological father slipped to the back of her mind. This evening, with classic ballads playing in the background, she found herself getting swept up in their words of love.

With the dinner dishes cleared and the tiramisu finished, Ric stood and held his hand out to her. "Would you care to dance?"

She glanced around. There was plenty of room on the outer deck. And then her gaze met his. The crooning ballad called to her. Ric had gone to a lot of effort. Why not enjoy every moment of this evening? Her problems would be waiting for her tomorrow. For tonight, she would enjoy the evening Ric had gone to such bother to plan for her.

He held his arms out to her, and she happily stepped into them. Her body fit next to his as though they'd been made for each other. As they moved about the floor, she leaned her head on his muscular shoulder and let her eyes drift shut. Instead of all the questions and worries that plagued her at night when she closed her eyes, right now, all she could think about was the strong, reliable man holding her so close.

She inhaled his spicy cologne. It mixed with his manly scent and made quite an intoxicating mixture. She breathed in deeper. A murmur of pleasure vibrated in her throat.

The truth was, they'd been dancing around each other since they'd met. The chemistry had arced between them since that first day in the garden of his uncle's villa. The first time he'd touched her, the tingles of awareness had zinged through her body. Since then she'd been fighting it. And right now, she couldn't remember why she'd been resisting him.

Ric was a good guy—strike that—he was a great guy. And she was so tired of fighting the magnetic pull that he had over her heart. Because with each morning coffee they'd shared, with each soul-searching conversation, with each heated glance, piece by piece he'd broken through the wall around her heart.

She stood there in his arms feeling utterly exposed and vulnerable. And at the same time, she felt liberated and excited to find out what would come next.

She once more breathed in his heady scent. Deeper. Longer. It must be going to her head because all she could think about was kissing him. Right here. Right now. And not just a peck on the cheek or lips. No. She longed for a deep soul-stirring, feet-floating-above-the-ground kiss.

But maybe she'd start with an appetizer. She moved her head ever so slightly and pressed her lips to the smooth skin of his neck. Immediately she heard the swift intake of his breath. She smiled. She wasn't the only one caught up in this evening of a dazzling sunset and twinkle of candlelight.

They stopped dancing. Experience had taught her that life could be short—much too short. And each moment had to be lived to its fullest. Gia decided to live daringly. She trailed kisses up his neck. She lifted up on her tiptoes. When she pulled back, their gazes met. There was passion ignited in his eyes.

And then she pressed her lips to his.

There was no hesitancy. There was need. Hunger. And desire. Oh, yes, lots of desire.

Her hands slid up, taking in the lines of his muscular chest. And then they slid over his broad shoulders. She tried to remember every feeling—every sensation—but every nerve ending of her body had been stimulated and her mind was on overload.

Her hands wrapped around the back of his neck. All the while, her lips were moving over his. His tongue delved inside her mouth. He tasted sweet like dessert wine. She didn't know if she'd ever drink that wine without being swept back in time to this delicious moment.

And then Ric swept her up in his arms. He took long, swift strides over to the navy-blue spacious deck lounge. Their lips parted as he gently set her down. And then he joined her.

Suddenly she turned shy. "Ric, we can't. Not here."

"Look around. There's no one to see us."

She glanced out at the black sea with just the moonlight dancing upon the water. "But what about the staff?"

"Trust me. We won't be disturbed." He leaned over and pressed his mouth to hers.

What was it about this man that had her doing things that she would never consider otherwise? Still, the thought of her and him beneath the stars seemed so fitting.

She wrapped her arms around his neck and drew him to her. She didn't need to dream tonight because no dream could be better than this moment with this amazing man, who had sneaked past her defenses and into her heart.

CHAPTER TWELVE

HAD THAT REALLY HAPPENED?

Oh, yes. It definitely had.

Ric smiled. The next day, he was still trying to wrap his head around the direction dinner had taken. Sure, it had been a quiet, intimate dinner, but he never imagined things would go that far. Okay. That was a lie. He'd definitely thought of it, but never really believed Gia would go for it.

Until now, Gia had been holding him at arm's length. Sure, they'd shared a kiss or two. But where they'd gone had been so much further than that. And now he had no idea where they went from here.

Before, they'd been two people helping each other get what they wanted—what they needed. She was helping him prove the merits of his program. And he was helping her locate her father. It was a clean, unentangled relationship. It was safe.

But now this thing between them was anything but safe. In one evening, she'd pulled back all the protective layers that he'd spent years wrapping around himself—to never be as vulnerable as he had been when his mother rejected him.

Now Gia had him thinking about life with her in it. When he thought of lunch, he wondered if she was free to have it with him. When he went home, he anticipated seeing her. She even had him bonding with Gin. That dog was an equal opportunity lover, who tucked Gia in at night but gravitated to Ric's bed sometime during the night.

Gia had stumbled into his life not so long ago and somehow in that short period of time, she'd managed to change everything. He felt off balance and not sure what to do next—with regards to his relationship with Gia—

Wait. Did they have a relationship? Was she expecting a commitment from him? His heart stilled. Did he want to make a commitment? His palms grew damp. In the past, the question wouldn't have materialized.

The questions without answers swirled in his mind, distracting him from work. Now he was pondering it. He was supposed to be answering an abundance of neglected and waiting emails. He had to do something while he avoided Gia— while he figured out what to say to her. Somehow, he couldn't imagine *Wow. The other night was awesome. We'll have to do it again sometime* going over very well.

No. Gia was much deeper than that. Relationships meant a lot to her. She took them seriously. If she didn't, she wouldn't be searching so hard for a biological father she'd never met. And she sure wouldn't be pinning all her hopes and dreams on it being a happy union—no matter that the man's past history said otherwise.

Gia was the type of person who couldn't help but walk around with her heart on her sleeve. She might try to hide it, but she wasn't very successful. And that's why when she'd looked at him in the morning light, after they'd made love, that he'd known he'd made a very big mistake.

Gia wanted a relationship. A real relationship with entanglements and emotions—all the things he'd been avoiding. And he had no idea what to do about it.

And now, when everything was so complicated, he'd gotten the phone call that he'd been waiting for—hoping for. Mr. Grosso wanted to meet with him that evening. And Mr. Grosso wanted him to bring along Gia to tell him how the program had helped her company.

Ric stared in the full-length mirror in his bedroom. His dark suit with a white shirt and burgundy tie exuded success and confidence, but he felt like a fraud. Sure, he was successful at business, but his personal life was in shambles. And where he was once quite confident, now he wasn't so sure he could be, or wanted to be, the man Gia wanted or deserved.

He checked the time. The last thing he wanted was to be late and give Mr. Grosso a bad impression of him from the start.

When he stepped into the living room, he was surprised to find Gia sitting on the couch with Gin, waiting for him. When their gazes met, she smiled. Not just a little smile, but a big one that lit up her whole face and warmed a spot in his chest. This wasn't good. Not good at all.

Stay focused on business.

Ha! That's easier said than done.

And then his gaze drifted lower, taking in the dazzling deep red dress that she'd chosen for the evening. His mouth grew dry. How was he supposed to focus on business when she was dressed like that?

When he stopped in front of her, she stood.

"You look stunning." Thank you."

Color bloomed in her cheeks. "Thank you."

Gin barked in agreement. They both laughed.

After Mrs. Rossi scooped up Gin and moved to the kitchen, they were alone. An awkwardness descended over Ric. He wasn't sure how to act around her.

"Shall we go?" He presented his arm to her. He told himself the gesture meant nothing.

She placed her hand in the crook of his arm. Her touch made his heart pick up its pace. This was going to be a long evening. Very long.

Everything is all right. It's just a very busy time. That's all.

It was what Gia had been telling herself since they'd made love and Ric seemed to have pulled away. At first, she told herself she was just imagining things. But as time went on, she noticed when he smiled at her, the smile didn't go the whole way to his eyes. What was up with that?

And she hadn't worked up the nerve to ask him about it. What if she was just seeing things that weren't there? What if she questioned his commitment to this relationship when he was already invested? She didn't want to do anything to rock the boat.

Maybe she was just expecting too much, too soon. After all, Ric was used to being a bachelor. He was used to doing things at his own pace. Now he not only had her in his life, but he also had an incorrigible dog living with him—who chewed on his good shoes if he forgot and left them out.

She just needed to slow down and let things happen naturally—even if it was slower than she'd like. They were fine. After all, if they weren't, would he have taken her on this very important dinner meeting?

What she hadn't anticipated was that they would be in a private room for dinner—just the two of them and Mr. Grosso. They were seated in a room that was obviously normally used for much larger parties than a party of three. When Ric said this man was a bit of a recluse, he hadn't been kidding.

Still, she couldn't dismiss the strange feeling of being in a big restaurant, but so alone. The murmur of voices reached them every time the server went in and out of the door. Gia wished they were out in the main room. Out there would be distractions that would perhaps put her more at ease.

She must not be the only one to feel the tension because Ric had been quieter than normal. He'd barely caught her gaze throughout the meal. He'd tried talking to Mr. Grosso, but the man wasn't talkative. At one point, the older man mumbled something about too much talk ruining a meal.

Okay, then why request a dinner meeting?

But thankfully the meal was almost concluded. She wasn't sure the mostly silent meal had helped Ric's sale. In fact, she was thinking it hadn't. And Ric must have felt the same way as the muscle in his cheek twitched like it did when he worked on his computer and something wasn't going right. Or when the dog wouldn't listen to him.

As the dinner dishes were cleared and their coffee was refilled, Gia decided to try to help Ric. "It was a lovely dinner. Thank you for suggesting we should meet here." Her gaze met the older man's. "We really appreciate you agreeing to meet with us. I'm sure once you hear about Ric's creation, you'll feel the same excitement about it that I do."

The older man's gaze moved between her and Ric. "How long have you two been together?"

Heat rushed to her face. She hadn't anticipated discussing her complicated relationship with Ric. "I haven't known Ric all that long."

"About the program," Ric intervened. "I have the real time results you'd previously requested."

The older man waved off the mention of business. He took a sip of his coffee and then leaned back in his chair. His gaze continued to move between the two of them. His gaze settled on Gia. "My Elizabeth was a lot like you. She was my biggest supporter." He sighed as though the memories were bittersweet. And then his gaze moved to Ric. "I just wish I'd have noticed her sooner—paid more attention to her."

Ric's jaw tightened. It was as though the man was trying to send him a message, and Ric wasn't having any of it.

Gia went for a distraction. "Is Elizabeth your wife?"

Mr. Grosso turned his attention back to Gia. "Yes. She was. Taken from me far too soon. When are you two getting married?"

"We aren't," Ric said. "Now about the program." He reached for his attaché, pulling out a manila folder. "I've brought some printouts that we can go over."

Mr. Grosso frowned and waved away the papers. "You two, are you a couple?"

"Yes," she said.

"No," Ric said.

They looked at each other after giving conflicting answers. Had she heard Ric correctly? After all they shared, it meant nothing to him?

His eyes were dark and filled with a swirl of emotions that she was unable to make out. Still, his answer hung there in her thoughts. Each time she recalled it, it was like a stab to her chest.

Their lovemaking meant nothing?

She meant nothing?

"Aw… See?" said Mr. Grosso. "I was right. There is something between you two." His attention zeroed in on Ric. "You're making a mistake by not marrying her as soon as possible. And trust me, you will regret it—"

"What I regret is not going over these reports," Ric said. "I think if you have a look at what I was able to do with my program to help Gia's business that you'll realize it will streamline and increase business for your company."

"I can't trust a man with my business who can't see what's right in front of him."

Ric raked his fingers through his hair. "Gia is not part of this business agreement."

"But she should be part of your life. When you are old like me, you'll find your business is a cold bed partner and a demanding mistress that never has enough of your time and always wants more, but never gives enough in return."

Ric was quiet.

Gia was still trying to wrap her mind around what was happening. Mr. Grosso was trying to be some sort of matchmaker. And Ric was denying that there was anything between them. And she was quiet because she didn't trust her voice right now. She didn't know which man she was most upset with.

After a tense moment, Ric said, "Would you like to see the reports?"

"I think I've seen as much as I need to." Mr. Grosso stood. "You get your life straightened out, and then we'll talk."

Ric stood. "My personal life has nothing to do with this." His words reached the man's retreating back. Once the man was gone, Ric turned to her. "Can you believe him?"

"What I can't believe is you." She grabbed her purse and followed in Mr. Grosso's footsteps.

"Gia, wait."

She kept going. She didn't want to have this conversation in the restaurant with witnesses. What she had to say to him, she didn't want overheard. And with the number of people gaping at Ric and pointing him out, she was certain a scene between them would make the headlines. That would just take a painful situation and make it unbearable.

Outside on the sidewalk, she turned the opposite direction of the valet.

"Gia, where are you going?" Ric rushed up to her.

She kept walking, stuffing down the heated words she had for him.

"Gia, please stop. Talk to me."

It was obvious he wasn't just going to let her walk away and find her own way back to the apartment. And so she stopped and turned to him. "What?"

His eyes widened as though he just realized what was going on. "You're mad at me?"

"You're sharp. No wonder you own your own business."

"Listen, about back there. I'm sorry. That man, he was over the top. I didn't realize he was going to talk about everything but business."

"Not everything."

Ric looked puzzled. "What?"

"Mr. Grosso didn't want to talk about everything, just about us. At which point you corrected him and told him there was nothing between us."

"Oh." Ric forked his fingers through his hair, scattering the short curls. "That's why you're mad."

"You bet it is." Her pride stopped her from admitting how deeply his words cut. "You didn't have the decency to tell me privately that our lovemaking was a mistake. Instead, you've been avoiding me. And then you blurt out to a stranger that it meant nothing to you."

"It's not like that."

She narrowed her gaze on him. "Then how is it?"

"I don't know."

"Don't know what?" She wasn't going to let him off that easy.

"I don't know anything. I wasn't expecting this, you, me and what's going on between us."

"Are you saying you want out? Or are you saying you were never into this thing between us?"

"What I'm saying is that I need time to process this. I need to figure things out. You are amazing." He reached out for her hand, taking it in his. His thumb rubbed over her skin. "Can you just give me a little time?"

She let out a pent-up breath. It wasn't the gushing admission of love she'd daydreamed about, but then again, it wasn't a big push-off either. It was actually a realistic approach to whatever this was between them. And maybe they both could use a little time to consider things.

She gazed deep into his eyes, finding nothing but honesty. "Time is a good idea."

His gaze searched hers. "You're sure? We're okay?"

She nodded. "We're okay."

He didn't release her hand; instead, he laced his fingers with hers as they walked back to get the car. She wasn't sure where they went from here.

It seemed like her life was becoming one big question mark. Would they find her father? Would things work out with her siblings? Would this thing with Ric lead somewhere?

Dinner had gone worse than he'd ever imagined. And the ride home was quiet and strained.

Ric's grip tightened on the steering wheel. Everything he'd worked for—everything he'd planned—was falling apart. How dare that man judge him and his work by his lack of a committed relationship? What kind of archaic thinking was that?

The only saving grace had been Gia's calm

presence. Through it all she'd remained pleasant, kept her cool and exuded a friendly demeanor. It was more than he could muster. Obviously that man had spent too much time alone, holed up in his mansion.

And then a worrisome thought came to him. Was he going to end up like Mr. Grosso? Old, alone and miserable?

He banished the thought. He liked his life. He was happy being a bachelor—not allowing anyone close enough to hurt him. He had nothing to worry about.

"I'm sorry about dinner," he said as they neared his apartment.

"The food was good."

"I meant the company." He wheeled into his parking spot.

"I'm sorry your deal fell through."

"I'm not." He never thought he'd say those words and mean them, but he did mean it. "I won't do business with someone so stuck in his ways." Ric's gaze met hers. "Thank you for being so good about everything."

"What will you do?"

"I don't know. I didn't have a backup plan because I thought I'd come up with the best pairing, his company and my program. I obviously thought he would be professional. I was wrong."

"You aren't giving up, are you?"

He raked his fingers through his hair. "You think I should try to work with that man?"

"Not necessarily him, but I'm sure your program can help another company."

She was right, even if he wasn't in the mood to hear it right now. At the moment, he just wanted to wallow in his disdain and anger. Sure, come tomorrow he'd see things in a different light. But for now, he just wanted to leave the subject alone.

Ric climbed out of the car and before he could round the car to get Gia's door, she let herself out. She was unlike the other women he'd dated. Gia wasn't helpless, but she could ask for help when she needed to. He admired her strength.

The more time he spent with her, the more he liked her. And he knew that was dangerous. Because when she tracked down her father, she would leave the island—leave him.

Unless he was to keep her at a friendly distance. He could do that. After all, it wasn't like he was falling in love with her. He could do the friends with benefits thing. He prided himself on being able to accomplish most anything he set his mind on. This wouldn't be any different.

CHAPTER THIRTEEN

SHE FELT BAD for Ric.

The meeting had been a total bust.

Gia wished there was something she could do to help him. But she knew absolutely nothing about computers, other than the basics. Programming was way beyond her abilities.

Still, she could tell Ric was going to be in a funk the rest of the evening if she didn't come up with a way to distract him. But what could she suggest that would keep him from heading back to his study where he'd grow even more melancholy?

When they entered Ric's apartment, the puppy came running up to them.

Arff. Arff.

"Does somebody need to go out?" Gia knelt and petted the little guy.

His tail rapidly swished back and forth.

"Okay. We'll go." She straightened and reached for the red leash on the black stand near the front door. It was then that she noticed Ric was lingering nearby and a thought came to her. "Would you like to join us for a walk?"

Ric shook his head. "That's okay."

It wasn't a direct no. In fact, it wasn't a no at all. And so she tried again. "It's a lovely evening. We could walk to the little gelato shop I spotted. I've been dying to try it. And then we could—"

She stopped herself before saying they could watch the sunset together. She was pretty certain that would sound like she was crossing the line between their arrangement to care for Gin and romance.

She told herself she had no room in her life for romance. She didn't even know who she was. Putting the brakes on this relationship was for the best. But she knew it was a lie. She'd fallen for Ric. Hard.

His dark brows lifted as though in question. "Could what?"

Heat rushed to her cheeks. The more she willed herself not to blush, the warmer her face became. "I don't know."

"Ah, but you do know."

If her face grew any warmer, she was quite certain her hair would spontaneously combust. "If you don't want to go—"

"Oh, I definitely want to go now. I just need to grab something."

Of course he would.

Without waiting for Ric, she attached the leash and was out the door in a jiffy. What was it about that man that could rattle her so much? Luckily, there was a light breeze. She welcomed the rush of air, even if it was warm.

"Hey, slow up," Ric called from behind them.

She supposed she couldn't act like she hadn't heard him, not after inviting him to join her. She pulled on the puppy's leash, getting him to slow down. Gia came to a stop. She refused to let Ric get to her. After all, he was just a guy—a sexy movie star sort of hunky man. And when he stared into her eyes, like he was doing right now, her knees went weak.

She waited for him to catch up to her. "Sorry. Gin is in a rush."

"Is it the puppy who's in the rush? Or is it you?"

She chanced a glance at Ric to find him smiling at her from under a navy-blue ball cap. So that's what he had to grab. Didn't he know that no hat could hide his good looks? And that sexy smile—was he flirting with her? Her heart picked up its pace as did her footsteps.

But she wasn't going to let him know he was getting to her. "Why would I be in a rush to get away from you? After all, I was the one who invited you on this walk, remember?"

"Oh, I remember. I also remember you blushing."

"Oh, you. You're insufferable."

At this point, he broke out in a deep, hearty laugh. This only made Gia blush more. She picked up her pace, not wanting him to see the affect he had on her.

At last they reached the park. As the puppy stretched its legs, Gia pretended to be intently interested in a red flowering plant. She would do anything to avoid Ric's inquisitive gaze.

"Are you going to ignore me after inviting me on this walk?" His words echoed her thoughts.

She stifled a groan and then proceeded to plaster on a friendly smile. "I was just intrigued by this flower. I don't think we have it in Tuscany."

He held out his phone and snapped a photo of the flower. "There. All taken care of. I'll have my assistant track down the plant for you."

She wasn't sure that was necessary. Still, she said, "Thank you."

She glanced at him before quickly turning away. Something had happened tonight. Maybe it was that man assuming they were a couple. Or maybe it was going to dinner with Ric as though it were natural for her to accompany him to important business meetings. Whatever it was, the delicate balance in their relationship was tipping over into the heart-pounding, staring-into-each-other's-eyes, kissing-like-there's-no-tomorrow area. And she'd just promised him time to figure things out. Why did this all have to be so complicated?

"Gia, wait." He reached out for her hand.

Her heart lodged in her throat. She stopped and turned to him. Her gaze met his once more. Did he know what she was thinking?

Ric reached out to her. His thumb gently caressed her cheek. A sigh whispered across her lips. All the while, their gazes connected.

She wanted to ask him what was happening. Where were they going to go from here? The words hovered in the back of her mouth, but her lips refused to cooperate. The words faded away.

When Ric's gaze lowered to her lips, she knew his thoughts had strayed to the same idea she'd had. He was going to kiss her. And in that moment, she wanted him more than she wanted anything else in the world—

"Hey, aren't you the guy from the movie?"

The voice was like a bucket of cold water thrown in the face. Both she and Ric pulled back as though they were doing something wrong. Were they doing something wrong? Had they been saved from making another mistake?

Her mind said one thing while her heart said something quite different. And right now, she didn't know which one to listen to because the pounding of her heart was too distracting.

Ric plastered on a smile, like the one he'd worn at dinner when Mr. Grosso had started going on about how a man who could invest in a long-term relationship was a reliable sort of man. Yeah, it was that smile.

"Can I help you?" Ric asked the young woman.

"Can I get a selfie with you? My friends are going to be so envious."

And so Ric granted the young woman one photo together. When it was over, Ric pulled his hat lower and added a pair of dark sunglasses.

"I don't think that's going to help," Gia said as they walked away.

He shrugged. "I don't know why I agreed to do that movie."

"Sure, you do. You thought it would be fun." At least she hoped that's the reason he'd done it.

"In truth, it was a bet and I lost. My friend starred in it and had producing rights. It was just supposed to be a small clip, no big deal. And then I don't know what happened."

She knew exactly what had happened. Most every woman on the planet who had seen the clip was now part of the Ric's fan club. Secretly she was a member too. Not that she'd ever admit it to him.

"Most men would die to be in the position of having women throw themselves at them."

"I'm not most men." Any hint of the smile that had been on his face was now gone, and in its place was a distinct frown.

"Why is that?" She shouldn't have asked. It was none of her business. And yet her mouth just kept doing its own thing. "Did someone break your heart?"

At first, he didn't respond. "It was something like that, but it's in the past. And now I have my career to focus on."

And here she thought she was the only one hiding behind a wall in order to keep from getting hurt. She sensed his wall was much thicker than hers and had been reinforced over years. How did one break down such a wall?

Deciding she needed to lighten the mood, Gia asked, "Would that be your acting career?"

He frowned and then shook his head. "A guy takes a sixty-second spot in a movie and everyone blows it out of proportion."

"Oh, but those sixty seconds were quite something." And then, because she couldn't resist teasing him, she asked, "So was that a body double? You know for those washboard abs?"

His lips pressed into a firm line as his brows drew together. "You know that was all genuine.

No stunt doubles were involved in the shooting of that scene."

Then, because she was having fun, she said, "I don't know if I believe you. You might have to prove it." When he reached for his shirt as though to rip it off and prove himself, she hurriedly reached out and grabbed his forearm, holding it in place. "Not that I wouldn't mind the show, but weren't you trying to stay under the radar?"

He glanced around, as though for a moment forgetting they were in public. "Yeah, right. But I was serious. It was me. All me."

She couldn't help but laugh as he stressed the point.

His dark brows drew together. "I'm serious."

"I know you are. That's what's so amusing." She couldn't stop smiling.

"I don't understand."

"It's okay. You don't have to." Men and their egos.

When they reached the gelato shop, it appeared they weren't the only ones to have the idea on this perfect summer evening. As they stood in a long line that stretched out the door, Gin drew people's attention. Passersby stopped to fuss over him, and the pup ate up all of the attention. There was no shyness when it came to Gin.

"Wait. Aren't you Ric Moretti from *Into the Sunset*?" a young woman asked.

"It is him," another young woman agreed.

"Hey, everyone!" the first woman shouted. "It's the hottie from *Into the Sunset*."

It all happened so fast that it caught both Gia and Ric off guard. One second they were standing beside each other, and the next there was a crowd forming around him.

Gia was shoved out of the way with such force that her foot landed on the edge of the sidewalk. She lost her balance. She flung her hands out to break her fall as she tumbled back.

She'd managed to turn herself midair and land on her hip. The air was knocked from her lungs. It took her a second to collect herself. Limb by limb she made sure everything was still working properly. Thankfully she could move everything.

When she went to stand up, Ric appeared in front of her. He knelt next to her. Concern etched across his handsome face. "Are you all right?"

"I think so. I just lost my balance." She struggled to get up.

Ric placed a hand on her shoulder, holding her in place. "Maybe you shouldn't move. I can call for help."

"Don't be ridiculous. I'm fine." She lifted a hand to him to help her up. It was then that she noticed the ugly red scrape on her elbow. "Just a couple of scrapes."

He took her hand in his. His grip was warm and steady. In no time she was back on her feet and feeling like a total klutz.

Ric lifted her arm and frowned at the oozing scrape and the cut on her palm. "We have to get you looked at."

She glanced around. A sinking feeling came over her. "Gin?" She continued turning in a circle; with each step her heart sunk lower. "Gin, come here. Gin?"

The puppy was nowhere in sight. How could she have let this happen? All she had to do was hold on to the leash. That was it. And yet she hadn't managed to do it.

Guilt pummeled down on her. Poor Gin. The little guy had to be so scared after that rush of people. But where could he have gone? She pulled away from Ric. She had to find the puppy.

"Gia, you need medical attention," Ric said firmly.

"What I need is to find Gin." When Ric didn't move, she turned to him. "Please. I can't go anywhere until we find him. He's scared and lost."

To her surprise, Ric didn't argue with her. He turned and started searching around their immediate vicinity. He walked to the nearby alley, looking behind garbage cans and in discarded boxes. She rushed over to join him. He looked on one side while she searched the other. No sign of the little guy. They retraced their steps to the park. Gin wasn't there either.

"I'll alert Marta," Ric said. "She can get people on social media involved. We'll find him."

Gia turned to Ric. "With his leash still attached, he could get hung up on something and not be able to get loose."

A rush of protective emotions pumped through her veins. She couldn't think of anything else but finding Gin, not even tending to her cuts and scrapes.

They kept moving—kept calling Gin's name. There was no sign of him. How could that be?

"Don't worry," Ric said. "We're not giving up. Maybe we should check the beach."

"I don't know," she said. Tears stung the backs of her eyes. "He wouldn't even know to go there."

"Actually, we go there almost every morning."

She blinked away the moisture gathering in her eyes. "You do?" When he nodded, she asked, "How do I not know this?"

"Because we go very early in the morning."

"While I'm still asleep?"

Ric nodded.

"Then let's go."

They race-walked to the beach. Gia called for Gin until her voice was hoarse. He wasn't here.

He wasn't anywhere they'd looked. And she was starting to wonder if she'd ever see him again.

The thought of never seeing that impish, loving puppy again was her total undoing. The world in front of her blurred. A tsunami of emotions engulfed her. Ric wrapped his arms around her. He held her as grief washed over her, leaving her raw and vulnerable.

She didn't know how much time passed when she pulled herself together. "I'm sorry about that. I didn't mean to fall apart."

"It's okay. I understand."

"But I'm not a crier. When my parents died, I didn't cry. When I found out I wasn't a Bartolini, I didn't cry. So why am I crying over a stray puppy that's not even mine?"

"That's a whole lot to hold inside."

"I'm strong. I'm a—" She stopped herself from saying she was a Bartolini like her…her father had taught her to say when she was young.

"Even strong people cry," Ric said.

"You don't."

He arched a brow. "How do you know that?"

She shrugged. "Ah…well, do you?"

They started walking along the beach as the sun set, sending splashes of color over the water. "I've cried," he said. "But I never told anyone because I was a jumble of emotions."

"What happened?"

Ric was quiet for moment. "It was a long time ago." His voice was soft as though his thoughts were caught up in the past. "The reason I'm so protective of my uncle and needed to prove he wasn't your father didn't have anything to do with his estate."

"You wanted to save his reputation?"

He nodded. "But more than that I needed to preserve the image that he wasn't like my mother—that he put other people's feelings ahead of his own."

"I take it you and your mother still aren't close."

Ric shook his head. "I haven't seen her in years. She prefers it that way and so do I."

"Wow. And here I thought I was the only one with parental issues."

"Trust me. You don't corner the market on parent problems."

"I'm here. If you want to talk about it."

He stopped walking and turned to her. "Has anyone ever told you how easy it is to talk to you?"

"No." A smile pulled at her lips. "But thanks for saying so."

Ric started walking again with her hand nestled in his. It felt so natural as though they were always this close. All the while, Gia's gaze searched their surroundings. She knew finding little Gin in this seaside city was a long shot, but she couldn't give up.

"My mother shouldn't have been allowed to have a child. She'd even tell you that herself. I was a mistake—one she reminded me about often."

Gia gasped. Not even her own mother ever mentioned in her journals that she thought of Gia as a mistake—even if she had been an unintentional result of an affair.

Not having anything positive to say about Ric's mother, Gia remained silent. This was his tale to tell. She was just here to listen—even though her heart went out to the image in her mind of Ric as a sweet little boy, a young child who didn't get the love he so rightly deserved.

"My mother wanted an easy life, and she was willing to do whatever it took—even sleeping with every man she thought could give her that lifestyle. And I just happened to be the result."

"But your father—"

"Didn't know about me. As I told you before, my mother doesn't even know who he is—if you can believe her."

"And you don't?"

He shrugged. "I think if she does know who it is, she's never going to tell me."

"But why wouldn't she tell you if she knew?"

He shrugged. "The only thing I can surmise is

that it would complicate her life—her very cushy life. The man she married when I was young didn't like kids. And that's how I ended up living with my aunt and uncle. Nothing was going to come between my mother and the lifestyle she thought she deserved."

"I'm sorry. I can't even imagine what that must have been like for you." She squeezed his hand tighter.

"After my aunt died, my uncle still hung in there—never giving up on me. I could tell that he wasn't thrilled to be a single parent, but he never pushed me out the door."

Ric stopped and turned to her. The sun's last lingering rays shrouded him in light. As she stood there looking at him, she saw him completely different now. And she knew why. That reinforced wall around him had come down. He let her see a vulnerable side to him that she never would have thought existed. And that made him even more attractive than ever before.

And then they were gravitating toward each other. She wasn't sure who moved first. Was it her? Or was it him? Either way, their lips met in the middle. Oh, did they meet. It was as though the stars in the sky had lit up just for them. Or maybe it was sparks of desire lighting up the evening.

There was no hesitation as his tongue delved

into her mouth. A moan swelled deep in her throat. He tasted sweet like wine. And she was already intoxicated by his touch.

She knew exactly where this passionate kiss would lead them. And in that instant, she didn't care about the right or wrong of it. She wanted to live in the moment. And that was a first for her.

In Ric's arms she was content—no, not content, exhilarated with the here and now. She wasn't worried about the past. And she wasn't anxious for the future and the answers she might find. Right now, in this moment, she had everything she could possibly want—and a little more.

She leaned into Ric. His muscular chest pressed against her soft curves. Could he feel the pounding of her heart? Did he know how he made her feel—

Buzz. Buzz.

The vibration of his phone in his pants pocket tingled her leg. It was like a wake-up call. This wasn't supposed to be happening. Not now. They had Gin to find.

Gia pulled away from him. She couldn't quite meet his gaze. The guilt of losing herself in the moment was too great for her.

"I'm sorry," Ric said. "I should get this. It might be news about Gin."

Gia nodded. She hoped it was good news.

Ric checked the caller ID and then pressed the

phone to his ear. "Marta, have you heard anything?" Silence ensued. "Where?" More silence. "Thanks. We'll check it out."

There was news. Gia's heart filled with hope. "What is it?"

"The puppy has been spotted, at least they think it's Gin, near the south shore."

"Really?" When Ric nodded, her mind started racing. "That's so far away."

"I sent them a photo of him. We'll know soon."

Gia retraced her steps. Her strides quick. Short. All the while, she was thinking. Where would Gin go? Someplace familiar?

Ric's phone dinged with a message. He frowned. "It wasn't him."

"I know where he went."

What happened back there?

As Ric maneuvered his car toward his uncle's villa, he replayed the scene on the beach. What in the world had gotten into him to open up about his past? He never spoke of that time.

It wasn't so much the pain of his mother's rejection—because he'd dealt with that long ago, when he told his mother to her face that he never wanted to see her again—but rather it was the vulnerability attached to the memory. Who admitted that their own mother rejected them?

And yet there was something about Gia that

made him want to comfort her—even if it meant revealing more of himself than he'd ever meant to. He cared about her. He knew that was a dangerous admission. The women he'd cared for in the past had hurt him deeply.

But Gia wasn't like those other women. She was kind, thoughtful and caring. If he had any doubts about that, they wouldn't be rushing to his uncle's place to find a stray dog that had stolen Gia's heart.

And then the memory of the kiss they'd shared on the beach came to mind. Okay, she was very special. But what happened when she found her biological father?

A frown pulled at his face. He knew the answer. She would leave here. She would return to the beautiful rolling hills of Tuscany and the boutique hotel that she ran. Her whole life was far from here. And everything he'd ever known—ever wanted—was here.

And he wasn't going to fool himself about a long-distance relationship. His assistant had tried that once before she'd met her husband, and it had been nothing but misery and loneliness. No, he wasn't going to subject himself to that.

"We're here!" Gia practically had the car door open before he pulled to a stop in front of his uncle's villa.

She didn't wait for him. She jumped out of the

car, calling the dog's name, and running to the back of the house. He was only a few steps behind her.

As much as he wanted to portray that he was strong and didn't get attached to people or things, there was something about Gin that had gotten to him. He didn't know if it was the sadness in the puppy's eyes when he wanted attention or the rapid swish of his tail when they were playing ball, but that dog was special, just like the woman who loved him—loved the dog that is.

And Ric was silently praying there was a reunion tonight. Because he didn't want to think of how crushed Gia was going to be if they went home without Gin. He refused to consider how he'd feel. He would be fine. He was used to people coming and going from his life. Oh, who was he kidding. He was worried. He missed the little guy.

He turned the corner of the house in time to hear, "Gin, there you are."

Gia was headed for the back corner of the garden that was only now partially cleared. What in the world would Gin be doing back there again? Ric would have thought the puppy would never return to the garden.

Gia knelt next to the spot where Ric had originally freed Gin from the wire. "Aw…"

What was she fawning over? The puppy? Ric

stepped up behind her and peered over her shoulder. He couldn't believe his eyes. He blinked, but it was still there.

A mirror image of Gin.

There were two of them.

"Where did he come from?" Ric asked.

"It's a she." Gia lifted her head and glanced around the yard that was still very much a work in progress. And then she pointed. "It must have come in and out of the hole in the fence. It's why no one has seen her until now."

Ric looked at Gin. "You didn't tell us you had a sibling." Then he frowned. "Do you think it has a home?"

She shook her head. "Nothing about her appearance says that she has a home. But the vet can check for a chip just to be sure."

"So we're keeping her?" Ric asked, already knowing the answer.

Arff. Arff.

Gia smiled. "Okay, Gin. We'll take her home too." And then realizing she hadn't actually consulted Ric, she glanced over her shoulder at him. "You don't mind, do you?"

His formerly quiet, spotless home was quickly being overrun by one messy but beautiful woman and one—scratch that, now two talkative dogs. Oh, boy!

"No, I don't mind." What was he saying? Of course he minded.

His home was his oasis from the craziness at the office. It was his sanctuary where he regrouped and strategized. And since Gia and Gin came into his life, he didn't know how lonely he'd been.

"Here." Gia held out Gin's red leash. "Can you hold on to him while I try to catch her?"

Ric took the leash. Gin came over to him and sat down without being told. He was a smart little guy. Now they'd see if his sister was smart enough to let Gia get ahold of her. That little dog had no idea what treats were in store for her. If she did, she'd leap into Gia's arms instead of running from her.

It took Gia a little bit, but finally she had her arms around the barking puppy. It was dirty and a bit on the thin side, but other than that she looked okay.

"Let's go home." Gia smiled.

He'd never seen her look happier. Who knew finding not one but two strays could make someone so happy? He supposed they both were rather cute. He smiled. And then he realized that Gia was rubbing off on him.

CHAPTER FOURTEEN

Ric wasn't the only one with contacts. Gia had some of her own.

And so after the disastrous dinner with Mr. Grosso, she'd made a phone call. Her mother's family had been vastly wealthy with old money. With great wealth came numerous contacts, and there was someone who had been in Gia's life as a child. He was more like an honorary uncle.

However, when she'd initially made the phone call to his office, as she didn't have his personal contact information after all these years, she was informed that he was out. So she'd left a message for him.

Today, he'd gotten back to her. He was willing to meet with her and Ric to discuss Ric's program. She hadn't given out any specific details about it, per Ric's prior request, just enough to pique the man's interest. But the catch was that they'd have to meet with him in Rome. Would Ric be agreeable?

She hoped to catch him before he left for work. She rushed out of her bedroom and practically ran into him in the hallway. She came to an abrupt halt on her tiptoes to keep from crashing into him.

His hands immediately wrapped around her waist as though to steady her. As her hands came to rest on his broad shoulders, her heart pounded harder. It was then that time seemed to suspend itself as they stared at each other.

They'd been here before, but it felt like a lifetime ago. She missed him touching her, feeling his lips move over hers. Her gaze dipped to his lips. It'd be so easy to lean forward and press her mouth to his. Every cell in her body longed to do just that.

And then she heard his voice echo in her head: *Can you just give me a little time?*

The memory cooled her mood. She pulled back, breaking the connection between them. She swallowed hard and struggled to regain her composure.

Her gaze didn't quite meet his. "I was just coming to find you."

"Funny. I was looking for you, too. I have news."

Her heart leaped into her throat. Could this be it? Could this be the moment she'd been waiting for what felt like a lifetime to hear?

"Is it my father?"

Ric smiled. "It is. We found him."

"You did?" She didn't wait for his response, she threw herself at Ric, wrapping her arms around his neck. Her body molded to his body as though they were two halves of a whole.

The jolt of awareness that zinged through her body snapped her out of her state of euphoria. And as much as she loved being this close to Ric, it wasn't right. He had to want her—all of her—before they could move in this direction.

She pulled back. "Sorry. I was just so excited. I was beginning to think this day would never come."

"It's okay. You don't have to apologize."

"Where is he? When can I see him?" She glanced down at her scruffy work clothes that she'd been planning to wear to paint the villa. "I can't meet him dressed like this. I have to change."

When she went to turn back to her room, Ric reached out, gently grabbing her arm. "Slow down. He's not here."

She turned back. "Where is he?"

"In Rome."

"Rome?"

Ric nodded. "He's a high-powered business banker."

"Then I need to book a flight—"

"No, you don't. We'll take my private jet."

"Are you sure?"

He nodded. "I already phoned ahead. It will be fueled and waiting for us."

"You're going with me?"

He nodded. "We've been through this whole journey together. I'd like to be there for you when it ends—or begins, depending on how you look at it."

"Thank you." Tears of joy clouded her eyes. She was about to meet her biological father. She was about to have a parent again. "Thank you for everything."

They agreed to leave for the airport in a half hour. It'd give Gia enough time to call her contractor and let him know she'd be away for a while—maybe forever if all worked out like she wanted. And it gave her time to pack.

Ric said that he would ask his housekeeper watch over the dogs. He said it wouldn't be hard, as the housekeeper had a soft spot in her heart for them. Seemed like the furry duo had everyone wrapped around their paws. They were so adorable.

Once Gia reached her room, she grabbed her phone. First, she texted her brother and sister, letting them know that she'd found her father—or rather that Ric had tracked him down. Her siblings sent good wishes, eager to know more about the man.

Next, she texted her family friend, letting him know that a spur of the moment trip was sending them to Rome and asked if they could meet for dinner. Her friend agreed and suggested tonight. She hesitated. Not sure how her first meeting with her biological father would go, she asked her friend if she could let him know later in the day. He agreed.

She couldn't believe it. Her biological father was finally found. Excitement pumped through her veins as she rushed around her room, packing all her stuff—unsure if she'd ever return.

But what if her father didn't want to know her? Fear clutched her heart. As quickly as the horrid thought came to her, she dismissed it. Things had to work out for the best. She needed to find her happy ending.

He was worried.

And he didn't know what to do about it, which was so unlike him. He was usually the man with the answers.

Ric chanced a glance at Gia as their hired car sped down the road toward her meeting with her biological father. She kept clasping and unclasping her hands. She was so excited. She was so certain this was going to be a happy union.

Ric had been down a similar road, not that he'd ever found his father. And that was the point. He'd been so certain if he wanted something bad enough that everything would work out. It hadn't.

And then he realized just because things hadn't worked out for him that it didn't mean they wouldn't for Gia. The truth was that he wanted her to be happy—for her dreams to come true. After all, one of them should have things work out the way they envisioned.

But he still couldn't help but worry that she'd set herself up for a fall. If that happened, he'd be there to catch her. He'd do everything in his power to make sure she was all right.

"Does he know he's meeting with me?" Gia's voice cut through Ric's thoughts.

"My assistant set up the appointment."

"No. What I mean is, does he know he's meeting his daughter for the first time?" Hope twinkled in her eyes.

Ric shook his head. "I thought you'd want to tell him yourself."

Gia paused as though to think it over. "You're right. It's best coming from me. I know it'll be a shock to him. It certainly was to me. But when he has a chance to absorb the information, I'm sure he's going to be as excited as I am."

"I hope so." Ric's gut twisted in a knot. He had a bad feeling about this.

Gia frowned at him. "Relax. It's all going to work out. You just have to believe."

"I'm trying. But maybe you should also be prepared, in case this doesn't play out the way you're envisioning."

Gia's gaze narrowed. Agitation threaded through her voice. "Why are you doing that?"

"Doing what?"

"Trying to ruin this for me?"

"I'm not. I swear. I just don't want to see you get hurt."

At that point the car pulled to a stop in front of a modern office building. The driver opened the rear passenger door for them. When they stepped onto the curb, they saw the man's name right there on the front of the building.

Gia rushed inside. Ric's long, quick strides kept up with her. After checking the directory on the wall, she pressed the button for the elevator.

Ric leaned close to her and whispered, "No matter what, I'm here for you."

She turned to him and smiled. "Thank you. For everything. This is going to be the best day of my life."

Or one of the worst. Ric kept the pessimistic thought to himself. Nothing was going to bring Gia's feet back down to the ground. Her head was filled with dreams of love, laughter and happiness. And he couldn't blame her. He just hoped the man they were about to meet didn't burst her bubble.

CHAPTER FIFTEEN

THE ELEVATOR MOVED so slowly.

And stopped at every floor.

Gia clasped her hands as she gazed at the floor numbers as they went by. Two more to go. Two more floors until she reached her biological father's office. Two more floors until she was able to right a wrong. She wondered what her parents would think of what she was about to do.

She halted her thoughts. She wasn't going to think about them. She wasn't going to think about the way they'd kept this vital information from her for her entire life.

She'd refused to think very much about her parents since she'd learned the truth about her conception. It was better that way. She didn't want to hate them. They had been good parents to her—more like great parents. Or at least she'd thought they'd been. But do great parents keep a secret of this magnitude from their child?

The elevator dinged as it stopped one floor

from her destination. They were almost there. Excitement bubbled up inside her. What was she going to say to this man?

She knew this was going to be a shock to her biological father. She shouldn't expect much at first, but she was certain he would quickly come around.

She'd used the time on Ric's private jet to plan out her words. She rehearsed them over and over in her head. She'd perfected them. This was going to work out just fine.

As the elevator moved to her final destination, she chanced a glance at Ric. His stance was rigid, and the muscle in his cheek jumped. He didn't come straight out and say it, but he thought this meeting was a mistake. He thought it was going to go terribly wrong. And she understood where he was coming from. He hadn't had the easiest childhood, and her heart went out to him. But this was different—they were different. It would work out. He'd see.

Because she couldn't afford to consider the alternative. If she let herself consider how wrong this meeting could go, she'd back out. She'd head back to Tuscany and always wonder what might have been. And when she stared in the mirror, she'd always wonder what aspects of herself had been inherited from her biological father.

The elevator stopped one last time, and then

the doors swept open. They stepped out on what looked like marble floors. A grand desk with a beautiful receptionist greeted them. Behind the woman, in big bold letters was her biological father's surname. Very impressive. He appeared to do very well for himself.

Gia stepped up to the desk. "Hi. Gia Bartolini to see Mr. Gallo."

The woman glanced down at the computer monitor. "Ah, yes. There you are. It'll be just a moment." She then spoke softly into her headset before returning her attention to Gia. "Mr. Gallo will be just a few minutes. Please have a seat."

"Thank you." Gia turned to find no expense had been spared in the waiting area. She took a seat in one of the burgundy leather chairs.

Ric sat beside her. "It's not too late to change your mind."

"If that's your attempt at a joke, it's not funny."

He didn't respond. Instead, he put his arm over her shoulders and then leaned in close. "You've got this. If he doesn't love you from the start, he's a very foolish man."

Now this was more like it. She turned to him, finding he was closer than she'd anticipated. "Thank you." She smiled. "Glad to see you're coming around."

Before he could say more, the receptionist interrupted. "You can go back now. It's the last door on the left."

Suddenly her insides melted into a ball of nerves. When she stood, her knees felt weak. She'd been doing so well. Why now? She had to get it together.

Ric stood and looked back at her as though wondering why she hadn't sprung out of the chair and raced down the hallway. She would, if her legs would cooperate.

His gaze met hers. "You've got this."

In his gaze she found strength. She drew on it, calming her rising nerves. She could do this. He presented his arm to her, she was tempted to hold on to him, but she resisted.

"I need to do this on my own." And then she walked ahead of him.

She wasn't sure if Ric was behind her as the carpeting was thick and muffled their footsteps. She thought of glancing back but decided it was best just to focus on her forward momentum, because no matter what she told herself, she was still nervous.

When she reached the closed wooden doors with Gallo's name on it, she paused. She drew in a deep breath and slowly exhaled it. Then she did it again. This was as calm as she was going to get. She raised her arm, folded her fingers and rapped on the door.

"Come in," said a deep male voice.

She realized in that moment it was the very first time she'd heard her biological father speak.

"You have to open the door," Ric whispered from behind her.

Oh, yeah. Right. Here goes nothing. Or everything.

She grasped the doorknob and turned. It was like having an out-of-body experience. For so long now, she'd dreamed about this moment. She wondered what this man would be like. And now it was happening.

She wasn't sure how her legs held her up, but somehow she made it inside the massive office without stumbling or totally falling on her face. The man was standing with his back to her. He had dark hair and was short in stature. She'd never imagined him as short. Not that there was anything wrong with it. It just wasn't how she'd pictured him.

And then he turned. He was clean-shaven. His suit was gray and obviously didn't come off a rack. He wore a blue tie that highlighted his blue eyes—so much like her own. But it was his mouth that drew her attention. He was frowning. Was he frowning at her? Or was that just his general disposition?

"You wanted to see me," Mr. Gallo said, not bothering to offer her a seat. "My assistant said it was a matter of importance, but yet I don't know you and we've never done business, have we?"

Gia's mouth was dry. Her tongue was stuck to the roof of her mouth. She swallowed hard, hoping when she spoke that she didn't betray her anxiety. "No." When he arched a brow, she continued. "We've never met."

"I didn't think so. I don't recognize the name, and I am good with names. I don't have much time so tell me why you insisted on seeing me."

Not exactly the cordial greeting she'd been hoping for, but it would change once she told him who she was. "I am Gia Bartolini. I... I believe you knew my mother, Carla Bartolini." When there was no recognition in his eyes, Gia realized perhaps that wasn't the name her mother had used when she met him. "Or perhaps you knew her as Carla Ferrari."

Still there was no recognition in his eyes. "I don't know you. And I don't know your mother. Is there a point to this meeting?"

"You're my father."

Oh, no! Had she just blurted it out? By the darkening look on the man's face, she'd say yes, she'd thrown the bombshell into the room.

And he didn't look happy. Not at all. She felt Ric move directly behind her as though to bolster her should she need it. But she could do this. After all, she'd anticipated that her biological father would be shocked at first. Who wouldn't be?

Once she explained, he'd understand. And so she started to explain about her parents dying and discovering the journal—

"Stop." His hand moved through the air as though cutting off her words. "I don't need to hear this. I'm not your father. If you came here for a handout—"

"A handout?" Was he serious? By the line of his brows, he was very serious. "I don't need your money. I have money of my own. I came here so we could get to know each other."

Mr. Gallo shook his head. "I'm not your father—"

"But my mother—"

"And I don't know your mother. Even if I did, that was a long time ago. I have my own family. I'm not looking for any strays."

Gia inhaled a swift breath. Did he just call her a stray? Tears pricked the backs of her eyes, but she refused to let this man—this horrible little man—see them.

"I must have made a mistake," she said, backing toward the door.

"That's more like it," Mr. Gallo said. "Don't come back looking for a handout. I'll see you in court first."

Gia turned and headed for the door. The rest

of the way out of the building was an utter blur. It wasn't until she was in the backseat of the car with Ric pressing a drink of water into her hand that she realized it was over. It was so over.

How could she have been so wrong? How could she be related to someone so cold—so miserable?

He wanted to make this better.

He wanted to stop the pain.

But Ric couldn't do either of those things for Gia. Why did he have to be right this time? He'd have been thrilled to be wrong—for Gia to get her happy ending.

He glanced over at her as she sat close to the door, leaving a huge gap of seat between them. Her face was turned to the window, taking in the sights of the city. He doubted she truly saw any of it.

His heart was breaking for her. She was stuffing all her disappointment and rejection deep down inside. He wanted her to open up to him— to tell him whatever was on her mind—but she'd become unusually quiet.

The best thing he could do for her was to get them home. He grabbed his phone from his pocket and texted his pilot, letting him know to ready the plane for a return trip. In the meantime, he'd just quietly wait for Gia to speak—if she'd let him in.

When the car pulled to a stop in front of their hotel, Ric joined her off to the side of the large glass doors leading to the lobby. Gia stopped there as though lost in her thoughts. It was only then in the bright Italian sunlight that he noticed the ghostly pallor of her face.

He moved in close to her, in case she wanted to lean on him or needed a hug. But he didn't make the first move. He didn't want to do anything that would cause her more stress.

"Don't worry," he said. "I contacted the pilot. He'll have the plane ready to go just as soon as you're ready to leave."

Gia nodded but didn't say a word. He wasn't sure if she really heard him. She was stunned and disappointed. Who could blame her?

She entered the hotel and headed straight for the elevator. On the way up to their suite, her phone dinged. She pulled it from her purse and checked the screen.

She turned to him. "We can't leave. Not before dinner."

Just then the elevator beeped as it reached their floor and the door slid open. All the while, Ric couldn't help but wonder what had changed. Why would she want to stay? There was no way that man had changed his mind about getting to know

Gia. It was totally his loss, as she was the most amazing person. Just her smile was enough to brighten up the world—at least, his world.

Ric used his keycard to let them in the suite. "Is there something you need to do before we leave?"

She nodded. "I'd like to meet an old family friend for dinner."

His gaze searched hers. She looked worn out and defeated. "Are you sure that's a good idea? Maybe another time would be better."

She shook her head. "I'm fine. You were right. I shouldn't have gotten my hopes up."

"I'm sorry. I never wanted to be wrong more in my life."

"I know." She sent him a smile, but it never reached her big beautiful eyes. "I'm just going to answer some emails and stuff until dinner."

"But what about lunch?"

She shook her head. "I'm not hungry."

"I'll order extra just in case you change your mind."

She was already walking away, leaving him alone with his thoughts. People seemed to think that having a lot of money could fix all of life's problems, but he'd be the first to attest that it couldn't. If it could, he'd give up his fortune to give Gia the family she wanted.

Being helpless was not a position he was familiar with. Usually there was something he could do—a plan to follow, a person to hire. But in this case, he had no choice but to sit by while Gia dealt with yet another big blow. First, her parents lied to her about her conception, and then that horrible man rejected her without even taking time to know anything about her. Life was not fair.

CHAPTER SIXTEEN

THEIR VISIT TO Rome hadn't worked out for her.

But that didn't mean it couldn't work out for Ric.

Because as disappointed as she was, Gia wanted Ric to find a good home for his program. She wanted his dreams to come to fruition for him, for herself—to reassure herself that sometimes dreams really did come true—and for all of the people it would help.

As they waited at the restaurant table for her friend, who'd texted to let her know he was running a few minutes late, Ric leaned toward her. "We don't have to do this. Not tonight."

"I'm okay." When Ric sent her a disbelieving look, she added, "I don't regret tracking that man down. And I don't regret meeting him."

"Even though he was an insufferable jerk?"

She nodded. "I now understand why my parents felt it was best to keep me from knowing about him. He's not a nice man—not someone

I want in my life. And so my parents did what they felt best because…" Her voice cracked with emotion. "Because they both loved me."

"I didn't know them, but from everything you've said and after knowing their amazing daughter, I believe they loved you with all their hearts."

Tears sprang to her eyes. She blinked them away, not wanting to make a show in public. "For the first time since they unexpectedly died, I'm no longer angry with them. I didn't realize until now just how angry I was with them for leaving me. I know the accident wasn't their fault and they in no way wanted to leave, but I was just so angry of being robbed of their presence in my life that I think I projected all that grief and anger into the secret of my conception. It was easier to be angry with them for keeping a secret than to be angry because they died."

Ric reached out, taking his hand in hers. No words were needed. His presence and show of support meant the world to her. If they were seated closer, she'd have leaned her head on his shoulder—

"Sorry, I'm late." The familiar gravelly male voice interrupted the quiet moment.

Gia and Ric withdrew their hands. She noticed the distinct coldness where just moments ago he'd been touching her.

She pasted on her brightest smile, as it was so good to see Vincent D'Angelo again. In a way, it was like having a piece of her parents back because they'd been such good friends with Vincent. In fact, they'd been so close that he was Enzo's godfather.

Vincent rounded the table. "Gia, I'm so sorry." The tall man with a broad chest enveloped her in a warm hug. When he pulled back, he said, "I was out of the country when I heard the news, and it was too late to make it back for the funeral."

"I understand. The flowers you sent were beautiful." She couldn't remember exactly which bouquet was his, but she recalled seeing his name on one of the many arrangements, and they were all stunning. She turned to Ric. "And I'd like to introduce you to m-my…" She stuttered, not sure what title to give Ric as their relationship was so complicated. And so she settled on "Ric Moretti."

Vincent leaned over and shook Ric's extended hand. "It's good to meet you."

Once they were all seated, they ordered pasta and made small talk, allowing the men to get to know each other a little.

And then Vincent turned to her. "It's been far too long. You remind me so much of your parents. You have your mother's beautiful looks and your father's easiness. I could always talk to him about anything."

His words were like a balm on her wounded heart. "You really think so?"

"I do. They were so proud of you. Any time I visited with them, they'd fill me in on all your accomplishments. You and your brother and sister were the highlights of their lives."

Gia genuinely smiled as memories of her parents crowded in her mind. They were caring and loving. She'd spent all this time searching for something she'd already had—parents who loved her. No one could replace them or their love.

And they weren't truly gone. They lived on in her heart and her memories. Instead of fighting the memories, she had to welcome them—accepting the pain of loss as well as the happiness found in those memories.

Gia turned to Ric. "Vincent owns a vast shipping company. It always has him on the road." Out of the corner of her eye, she caught Vincent nodding in agreement. "I thought you two could help each other. He could certainly use your program, and he has a stellar reputation in the transportation community. And I might have mentioned your ultimate goal is to use your program to help get supplies to those in need."

"Yes, she did," Vincent said. "I am very interested in hearing more."

Ric glanced at her. His eyes were dark and unreadable. It was as if suddenly a wall had gone up between them. But she told herself it was just the surprise she'd sprung on him. Everything would be all right in the end.

Ric was hesitant to reveal much at first, but Vincent just kept talking. No wonder he was so successful at what he did. He could talk most everyone into seeing things his way. And though Ric was hesitant at first, the more Vincent talked, the more Ric talked.

Gia smiled. This was all going to work out.

What had happened?

Gia had planned this without mentioning it to him.

Throughout the dinner, he'd avoided eye contact with her. He felt as though she'd somehow betrayed him, but he'd done his best to hold it all in during the meal—a meal he'd barely tasted.

Ric had promised to meet with Vincent again to go over details of his program and show him what it had done on a small scale for Gia's boutique hotel business. But he wasn't happy about it. Still, he was a businessman first, and this was an opportunity that he just couldn't ignore—even if he wanted to.

Because this was a pity offering.

Gia didn't believe in him enough to think he could pull off this project on his own. It reminded him of his mother.

But in spite of everything, he'd made a success of himself—a self-made man.

Gia didn't get to take that away from him. Sure, he might have had a setback with Mr. Grosso, but he hadn't given up. He had other options. He just hadn't had time to explore them.

On the ride home, Gia tried to make conversation, but he wasn't in the mood to speak, only giving her a nod or one-word answer.

It wasn't until they were in their suite that he turned to her and asked, "What have you done?"

Her eyes widened with surprise. "I... I was helping you."

"I don't need help! I can manage my business fine on my own."

Anger flared in her eyes. "So you can help me, even though I didn't ask you to, but when I return the favor, it's wrong?"

He raked his fingers through his hair. "It's not the same thing."

"What's the matter? Your ego can't accept the help of a woman? Or is it just this particular woman that you won't take help from?"

A tangle of emotions churned within him. "I don't need your help."

"Good. Because I don't need you either. I don't need anyone." She turned and strode away.

He watched her walk away, leaving him alone once more. Loneliness engulfed him. Refusing to go after her, he retreated to his room. His door shut with a loud thud. It was time to go home.

This trip had been an utter disaster. The one person who he thought believed in him had just turned her back on him, like so many others in his life. He was better off on his own.

Gia regretted her words.

As she threw her things in her suitcase, she realized she was acting just like her biological father—whom she wished she'd never met. The man was selfish and self-centered. She wouldn't turn into him.

Her thoughts turned to her brother and sister. She'd left them to pick up the pieces of her life back in Tuscany when she'd dropped everything to go on this journey of self-discovery. Not wanting to be anything like the man she'd met that morning, she knew the time had come to return home as soon as possible.

And though it broke her heart, she realized that Ric wasn't going to make room in his life for her. He'd been putting off telling her since they'd made love. She knew it then, but she'd been hoping she was wrong. Just like she'd been hoping her biological father was someone she'd want to know. She was wrong in both cases. No man could love her.

With a hole in her chest where her heart had

once been, she rolled her suitcase into the common room. Ric was there, checking his phone. He glanced up when she entered. "Good. The plane is ready to go."

She shook her head. "I'm not going back with you."

He opened his mouth to say something, but then changed his mind, closing it without saying a word. And that right there said it all. She was doing the right thing—for both of them.

Tears pricked her eyes, but she blinked them away. She would get through this without breaking down. It was for the best. That's what she kept telling herself. But there was nothing about this departure that felt like it was for the best.

Returning to Lapri would be just too hard. She needed—they needed—to make a clean break. "I'm returning to Tuscany. Tonight."

"And the puppies?"

She loved them nearly as much as she'd thought she loved Ric. But if she were to take them, Ric would have no one. He'd be alone except for his work. They might not belong together, but that didn't mean she wanted him to be alone.

Whereas when she returned to Tuscany, she had her family. Their importance in her life had gotten overlooked with the revelations of the journal, but it was like the blinders had been lifted from her eyes. She remembered how much Enzo and Bianca meant to her. She wouldn't forget again.

"You...you keep them. They are devoted to you."

She didn't know what she expected him to say, but he said nothing.

She clutched the suitcase. This was it. This was the last time she would ever see him. And yet she didn't have the strength, the courage to lift her gaze to his. She knew once she did that the wall she'd built up, damming up her emotions, would come crumbling down. She would be a wet, blubbering mess. And that was not how she wanted to end things.

"Thank you," she said, trying to maintain a level voice. "I appreciate everything you did for me. As for the villa, it's nearly done. I'll be in contact with the contractor about the final details."

Still, Ric said nothing. He was not going to make this easy for her.

After asking him to forward her other pieces of luggage, she turned and headed for the door. She didn't know what she expected—perhaps for Ric to come after her and ask her to stay. Not that it would be good for either of them. But he didn't speak. He didn't move. So she just kept going. Walking right out of his life. And she had never known such misery.

CHAPTER SEVENTEEN

HOME AT LAST.

Gia didn't know how she'd feel when she returned, but it felt good to walk through the doors of the villa. Because no matter where she went in this world, returning to the Bartolini estate for her was still coming home.

And right now, her broken heart needed the comfort of this place. She didn't know what she'd expected when she left here almost two months ago. She felt like a totally different person but not in a good way.

She felt as though she'd aged ten or twenty years. She was disillusioned, disheartened and wanted to disappear. She'd wanted to avoid the main house, but she needed to grab her keys from the office. She'd left them there for safe-keeping.

It was late enough in the evening that she hoped to avoid everyone, including her big brother. She just needed time to think—to settle back into her life…without Ric or the puppies. Another wave of sadness struck her.

She heard some laughter. And then a woman said, "I think your wine is a winner. The best I've ever tasted."

"You don't have to say that." Enzo's voice trailed down the hallway.

"No. I mean it. You were definitely born with a gift to run the vineyard."

When the couple stepped into the kitchen, they came to a halt. The other voice belonged to Sylvie, the wedding planner. And these two looked really comfortable together. Obviously, Gia had missed more than she'd thought while she was away.

"Hello, Enzo. Sylvie."

Was her brother blushing? Impossible. He didn't blush about anything, but then again, she'd never caught him with someone he was attracted to. Interesting. Very interesting.

"Gia, what are you doing here?" Enzo's voice held a note of irritation.

Was he upset that she was back? Or was he upset because she'd interrupted something? Gia was willing to go with the latter. And as much fun as it'd be to tease her brother about this thing with Sylvie—if there was a thing—she just wasn't up for sibling banter.

She was beat from traveling. She was torn up

just the rejection of one

nought of Ric caused the

g with unshed tears. She

oping her voice wouldn't

it emotions. "I just got

you two—"

t," Sylvie said. "In fact,

go. It's good to see you

at Sylvie made a quick

o return. At last."

nd of Enzo's voice. Her

h guilt for abandoning

er known to go off on a

arent who wanted abso-

h her—who'd have been

now she existed.

other, prepared for his

. She'd handled things

ut knowing she wasn't

to meet his. "I'm sorry,

this time."

was no anger—no re-

Only a brotherly love.

me. You were missed."

anding and caring crum-

to keep her emotions in

check, and she rushed forward and he wrapped her in a big bear hug. She couldn't believe she'd run away when she had everything she'd ever need right here. This was her family. She may not have Bartolini blood in her, but that hadn't stopped her father from loving her. She had been his daughter by choice, and that meant the world to her because he didn't have to love her but he did anyway.

Gia pulled back and swiped at her damp cheeks. "I'm sorry. I'll do better."

Enzo searched her eyes. "You don't have to apologize. It wasn't fair what you've had to go through. I just wanted to be there for you."

Fresh tears spilled onto her cheeks. "Have I told you lately that you're the best big brother?"

"No. But it's about time you realized it." He sent her a teasing smile. "I thought you weren't coming back for a few more weeks."

"Things changed." Her thoughts turned to Ric, and the pain in her chest still felt raw. She wasn't ready to talk about him. "I'm going to bed. Good night."

"Night."

"Gia?"

Who was calling her name?

She wasn't ready to wake up. Gia snuggled farther under the downy soft duvet. She struggled to return to her dream—her nice dream—her sexy dream.

Ric was there in her dreams. He'd been smiling at her, laughing with her, flirting with her and kissing her. She moaned. Where was he now? She searched through the foggy recesses of her dreams—

"Gia?"

Gia grunted. She didn't want to wake up, she wanted Ric back.

"Gia, I have coffee."

A whiff of coffee reached her nose. It was a jolt to her sluggish body. That did it. The dream was over. Like Pavlov's dog, her mouth watered at the thought of coffee. What could she say? She loved the stuff.

And when she opened her eyes, she found the coffee and voice weren't part of another dream. Bianca stood there holding two steaming mugs of coffee.

"Hey, sleepyhead. I thought you were going to snooze the day away."

And then everything came rushing back to her—the reason she'd returned to Tuscany early. Now she wished more than anything that she was still sleeping.

"Here." Bianca held the mug out to her. "Maybe this will help."

Gia shimmied into a propped-up position

and gladly accepted the coffee. She pressed the warm mug to her lips and practically inhaled the creamy brew.

Once she'd swallowed, her gaze returned to her sister—her sister who would soon be a bona fide princess. She was all done up, from her white-and-turquoise-striped skirt and white blouse to her hair, which was twisted at the back of her head and pinned up with loose corkscrew curls to soften the look.

"What are you doing here? Shouldn't you be in Patazonia?" Not giving Bianca a chance to respond, Gia asked, "And why do you look so fancy this early in the morning?"

"It's not early. In fact, it's almost lunchtime. And I had planned to return later this week to help Sylvie, but then Enzo called last night. And, well, I hopped on the jet and here I am."

"On your private jet. Must be nice."

Gia was still wrapping her mind around her sister's life turning into a real-life fairy tale, including the evil mother-in-law. Okay, maybe evil was too strong. But the woman had certainly not made things easy for Bianca. But the queen didn't know her sister like Gia did. Bianca never ever gave up on the people she loved. And she loved Leo with all her heart.

"I'm not here to talk about me. I want to know what's going on with you."

"I can't believe Enzo ratted me out." And then she recalled her run-in with him and Sylvie. "Is there something going on with Enzo and Sylvie?"

"Ah...not that I know of. But I'm not here all that much. Why? What did you see?"

Gia shrugged and then took a sip of coffee. "It's not what I saw as much as a vibe I was getting. But then again, I was really tired last night. Maybe it was nothing."

"I don't know, but what I want to hear about is you and what happened in Lapri."

"I don't want to talk about it." Gia drank more coffee as she avoided her sister's narrowed gaze.

"Don't want to talk about what?" Enzo stood in the doorway of her bedroom.

The gang was all here now, and Gia knew there was no way she'd be able to make it to the shower until she told them everything about her journey to find her biological father. She didn't blame them for being curious. If she was in their shoes, she'd be dying to know what had happened.

And so, with Bianca settled on the other side of the bed with coffee in hand, and Enzo perched on the end of her bed, Gia drew in a deep breath. She could do this—so long as she didn't mention Ric or the puppies she missed so dearly.

Gia told them about the dead ends she'd faced trying to find her father. And about Ric's friend who was able to glean information from the journal that she couldn't see. Then she came to the tough part of the story—about how her biological father was nothing like she'd imagined. She'd been so wrong about him—about their parents.

"Now I understand why our parents kept the truth from me—from us. They weren't trying to keep us apart, they were trying to shield me from a very selfish man. I don't know if I'd have made the same decision as them, but I hope I never have to find out."

"They loved you." Bianca leaned over and hugged her.

Enzo placed a hand on her lower leg. "We love you, sis. And we'll always be here for you. No matter what. We're Bartolinis, and Bartolinis stick together—through thick and thin."

Tears of love and gratefulness rolled onto Gia's cheeks. "Thanks, guys. You two are the best."

While Gia swiped away the tears, Bianca asked, "So what's the deal with Ric? Did you leave early because you found out your biological father isn't who you thought he'd be? Or did something happen with you and Ric?"

That was Gia's cue to get out of bed. "There's nothing to talk about."

"When she says that—" Bianca looked at Enzo "—it means she left the best part out."

Enzo didn't say anything, but he looked at her with those observant eyes of his.

resh clothes from the
e shower. "Just leave it

bathroom door. It was
her tears. She'd made
e'd risked her heart not
n rejected both times.
ust a man again. Except
He was her big brother.

CHAPTER EIGHTEEN

TIME MARCHED ON.

And he was more miserable with each passing day.

Ric held the leashes of the pups as he walked them to the park where Gia used to take them. Even the dogs weren't themselves since she left. They missed her too.

He'd been telling himself that he didn't need Gia in his life—that he'd be fine on his own. It didn't matter how many times he told himself that though; it didn't make it any truer.

He'd gone back to working long hours. He'd put a hold on the remodel of his uncle's villa. He'd picked up everything that reminded him of her in the apartment and placed it all in her room. He closed the door on it. Out of sight, out of mind. Ha! That just wasn't the case.

He thought of her in the morning when he went to the kitchen and found that she hadn't beat him to the coffee. He thought of her at lunchtime when he thought of sneaking out of the office to surprise her with a picnic lunch at his uncle's villa, where she'd been turning it from a rough stone into the true polished gem it could be. He thought of her when the pups whined at him and he had no clue what they were trying to say, but Gia would know—she had that way with animals and humans alike.

And he thought of her when Vincent D'Angelo had given him a follow-up phone call, wanting to know more about Ric's program. In fact, they'd already met to go over the details. They were even moving into negotiations for the rights to the program.

And though his program was at last going to be sold and open the door to help others, he didn't have a feeling of accomplishment—of fulfillment.

He sat down on a park bench. The pups sat on each side of him. When they used to come to the park with Gia, they'd beg to go play with the other dogs, but not anymore. Nothing was the same for any of them.

They all missed Gia.

And it was his fault.

He'd let his ego get in the way. He was a foolish man. How could he think Gia was doing anything other than what she always did—lending a helping hand? He'd measured her by the standards of the other women who'd passed through his life, and that wasn't fair to Gia.

There was only one thing to do.

Ric looked at the dogs, who sensed something was up and stared back at him. "Who wants to go find Gia?"

A round of barks ensued.

It was unanimous.

Ric pulled his phone from his pocket and called his pilot. They were leaving for Tuscany as fast as Ric could make the necessary arrangements. For the first time since Gia left, he smiled.

He stood. "Okay. Let's go get Gia and beg her to forgive me."

They barked in agreement before pulling on the leashes to go home.

They had packing to do.

Hours later, they'd arrived.

Ric and the two pups walked up to the door of the Bartolini Hotel. It was charming, just like the online photos had portrayed. He expected nothing less after getting to know Gia.

He stepped inside. A tall man was passing through the spacious foyer. He paused and glanced up. "Welcome to the Barto Villa. Can I help you?"

"I was hoping to speak with the woman in charge."

"Do you have a reservation?"

"No. I don't."

"I'm afraid we're fully booked. I can give you the name of another hotel—"

"If I could just speak with Gia."

"She isn't available." The man's dark brows drew together. "Do you know her?"

Isn't available? What did that mean? If she wasn't working, where would she be?

A young woman entered the room. Her attentive gaze moved between him and the man frowning at him. Ric wasn't sure what he'd done to set off the man.

"Can I help you?" the woman asked.

Before Ric could answer, the other man spoke. "He's looking for Gia."

The woman's gaze moved to the dogs before returning to meet his gaze. He couldn't tell what she was thinking. "You're Ric, aren't you?"

So, Gia had told them about him. Interesting. "Yes, I am. If you could just tell Gia I'm here—"

"No." The man crossed his arms over his chest.

"Then tell me where she is and I'll go to her."

"No," the man said again.

This guy certainly didn't like him. So was this guy interested in Gia? Or was he the protective older brother? Ric studied the man. The eyes were similar to Gia's. Ric was willing to bet this was her brother. And if that was her brother—

he glanced at the woman with similar colored eyes—she was most likely the sister.

"Why do you want to speak with our sister?" the woman asked.

So he was right.

"What does it matter?" Enzo asked. "He had his chance and he blew it."

Bianca frowned at her brother. "Would you let him speak?"

"Won't matter. I don't care what he has to say. He's not going to hurt Gia again."

A smile tugged at Ric's lips though he resisted the urge. He loved that all along Gia had the family that she'd desired just waiting for her. It may not be the father she'd envisioned, but her brother and sister clearly loved her fiercely. Now he just had to convince them that he was here to fix things.

"I don't want to hurt your sister. I swear." Ric searched for anything that would remove the frown from Enzo's face.

Bianca studied him. "I believe him." And then she approached Ric. He wasn't sure what she was going to do until she knelt to fuss over the dogs. "Aren't you two cuties?"

"I don't believe him." Enzo stood there with his arms crossed, not budging at all.

"Just give me a few minutes to speak with her. If she wants me to leave after hearing what I have

y didn't want to have to
brother, but he wasn't
ith Gia.

he turned to her brother.
u tried to stop me from
w that turned out." She
e're getting married at

big brother, he's a bit

d. "Fine. You can talk to
she tells you to."

these cuties while you
r hand for the leashes.
ver. "Thank you." He
o still didn't look happy.

cted him to Gia's house
oped Gia wasn't as stub-
Because she'd stolen his
nagine life without her.

CHAPTER NINETEEN

WHEN SOMETHING WAS bothering her mother, she would clean.

Gia decided to follow her mother's example, and she set to work cleaning her one-bedroom house. She should be working at the hotel as Ric's program had once more filled their reservations for the near future and beyond, but her manager, Michael, appeared to have everything under control. And he knew to call her if anything came up.

Gia had stripped her bed that morning. Now her linens were fresh and the bed was made. After cleaning and dusting the bedroom and bathroom, she'd moved into the living room. She'd had to borrow a ladder from the main house to reach the curtains. She hadn't decided if they needed dusting or something more drastic.

Knock. Knock.

"Come in," she called from atop the ladder.

She heard the door open and footsteps. She fully expected it to be her brother or sister. It seemed they were taking turns checking on her. How many times did she need to tell them that she was all right until they believed her?

"Gia?"

That voice. That was Ric's voice. Ric was here?

She spun around. She moved too fast. The old wooden ladder lurched to the side. Her body followed the ladder.

And then Ric was there. He braced the ladder with his arms. She'd rather his arms were around her. As soon as the thought came to her, she dismissed it. She refused to let him see that his nearness got to her.

She lowered herself to the floor before lifting her gaze to meet his. "Ric, you shouldn't be here—"

"We need to talk."

She shook her head. "We said everything that needed to be said back in Rome."

His eyes pleaded with her, pulling at her heartstrings. "Just hear me out."

Her mind said no. She couldn't risk being hurt again. But her heart urged her to listen to him. Torn between the two, she closed her eyes and shook her head, attempting to clear her mind.

"I'm so sorry, Gia." His deep voice was so close. "I was wrong."

What exactly was he saying? For so long she'd been making things up in her head the way she'd wanted them to be, and that had brought her nothing but pain. This time she wasn't going to jump to conclusions. This time she needed Ric to spell everything out to her, clearly and with no gray areas.

She opened her eyes and turned to face him. When his sorrowful gaze met hers, her heart leaped into her throat. How was she supposed to resist him when he looked at her with those sad puppy eyes?

She swallowed hard. "About what?"

"I was wrong to think I didn't need anyone in my life." His gaze searched hers. "I was wrong to accuse you of not believing in me."

His words were what she'd longed to hear. "I've always believed you could do anything you set your mind to. I just wanted to help. I never meant to make you doubt yourself."

"It wasn't you. It was me. I thought I was past those old insecurities from when I was young, but I guess they're still there lurking in the shadows. Will you forgive me?"

Gia bit back the yes that rushed to the tip of her tongue. She wasn't willing to let him off the hook just yet.

As though he sensed her inner struggle, Ric said, "I need you in my life. I've missed your smile. I've missed your coffee. I've missed our talks. I've missed everything about you."

Gia stared up into Ric's eyes. If she had any doubt about his feelings, they were quickly put to rest as the love was right there for her to see.

She had some of her own explaining to do. "I've been searching for my biological father because I thought he was the only true family I have left." Her voice grew thick with a rush of emotions.

"Gia—"

She shook her head. "Let me finish." She quickly gathered her thoughts and searched for the right words. "I was so hurt when my parents died and then when that journal turned up, taking away what was left of my family. I've never been so lost—so hurt. And then you came along. You didn't try to stop me from finding the truth. Instead, you helped me. You were by my side the whole time. Thank you for that. It meant so much."

"There's not any other place I'd rather have been."

She needed to tell him the rest. It was too important not to say it all.

"But when I found my biological father, it was not what I'd imagined. In fact, it was quite the opposite. I was so devastated that it took me a bit to regain my balance. But I have now, and you know what I figured out?"

Ric stared deep into her eyes. "What?"

"I didn't need him to complete me. My parents didn't tell me about him because they didn't want me to be hurt. My parents loved me. And I always had a father. He may not have been of the same blood, but that just means his love for me was so great that it superseded any biological connection, and for that I am grateful." Tears of joy and of loss spilled onto her cheeks.

Ric swiped away her tears. "I didn't know your parents, but after getting to know you, I have to believe they were good and loving people. They only wanted the best for you."

"I know that now. I know that I still have my family. I never lost them. My siblings are still there for me and I for them. And my parents are right here." She placed her hands over her heart. "It just took me a bit to realize all of this."

Ric smiled at her. "I'm happy for you."

"And there's one more thing I realized."

"What's that?"

"How much I love you."

Ric's smile broadened, lighting up his eyes. He reached out and drew her to him. "I love you too. You are my family."

More tears spilled onto Gia's face—tears of an overabundance of love. She placed her hands on his firm chest as she lifted up on her tiptoes—

Arff! Arff!

The echo of barks filled the room. They both turned to find two happy puppies running toward them through the open door.

Gia turned to Ric. "You brought them?"

"Of course I did. I wasn't the only one who missed you. And I wasn't taking any chances. If you turned me down, I was going to pull out my secret weapon—puppy kisses." Ric stared into her eyes. "I would do anything for you."

Gia leaned into his arms and their lips met. His touch sent her heart soaring. She would never tire of his kisses—just as she would never get enough of them. How had she gotten so lucky to find Ric? Now that she had him, she was never going to let him go.

Arff! Arff! Arff!

The puppies pawed at their legs, wanting some attention.

Ric and Gia pulled apart to look down at their adorable family. She could hardly believe this was happening. Her life was overflowing with love, from the enduring passionate kind to the furry adorable kind. The puppies fussed to be picked up.

She laughed. "Bringing the puppies for backup definitely would have worked."

They both knelt. Each picked up a puppy and then straightened. As though on cue, Blossom—she'd named the female dog before they'd left for Rome—stretched up and licked Gia's cheek.

"I see you weren't kidding about the puppy kisses."

"I'd never joke about something that important. I just don't know how they got down here," Ric said as he ran a hand down over Gin's back. "I left them with your brother and sister at the hotel."

Someone cleared their throat rather loudly.

"That would be our fault," the familiar female voice said.

Both Gia and Ric focused on the doorway where Bianca and Enzo now stood.

"Hey, guys." Gia smiled. In fact, she couldn't stop smiling.

Bianca smiled back. "I guess we don't have to ask how this is going to work out."

"We came to our senses," Gia said.

"Yes, we did," Ric chimed in with one arm holding Gin while his other arm was around Gia's waist.

The only one not smiling was Enzo. "I suppose this means you'll be going back to Lapri with Ric."

Gia turned a questioning gaze to Ric. "We hadn't talked about it yet, but there is this beautiful seaside villa that I'd love to finish fixing up." And then a worrisome thought came to her. She met Ric's gaze. "That is, unless you sold it."

He shook his head. "I saw the way you looked at it. I knew it right away, even if I wasn't ready to accept the fact that it would one day be our home."

Gin barked in agreement.

She turned back to Enzo. "Looks like you've won the estate."

Her brother didn't smile.

"Yeah," Bianca chimed in. "You won't have us butting into the business. You can change things to the way you want them."

"But if you want to keep them the same," Gia said, "both Michael and Rosa can take over the hotel aspect."

"And Sylvie is marvelous at planning weddings," Bianca added.

"It just won't be the same," Enzo said.

Who'd have thought their strong, unemotional brother would have a hard time with them both leaving? Gia felt guilty for being so excited about this new direction in her life.

"I'm sorry," Gia said.

"I am too," Bianca said. "We don't mean to leave you all alone here. But we'll be back to visit. Won't we?" Bianca's gaze moved to Gia.

"Yes, we will. In fact, we'll be here so much that you'll get sick of us."

Enzo shook his head. "Don't worry about me. I'll be fine. I just want you two to be happy. It's what our parents would have wanted."

"We want the same thing for you." Gia handed Ric the puppy.

She walked up to Enzo and hugged him. Bianca joined them. At last the tension was gone and they were back to being themselves.

When they pulled back, Gia returned to Ric's side and took the squirming puppy from him. She turned back to her brother. "What are you going to do with the villa now that it's all yours?"

"I don't know. I'll give it some thought when I fly to Paris. I'm attending a wine competition."

"That sounds exciting." Gia smiled, hoping her brother would do the same.

He did, but it didn't quite reach his eyes.

Enzo was about to head off on his own journey, and she wished him the very best. She knew change came with its own sets of bumps and unexpected turns. She was sure when it was all over, he would be happy to be the sole owner of the estate. Their father would be proud to have Enzo in charge. Somehow, she had the feeling things were going to work out just the way they were supposed to.

She returned to Ric's side. Oh, yes, they were definitely working out just right.

Then Ric leaned over to her and whispered in her ear, "I love you."

"I love you too."

* * * * *

If you missed the previous story in
The Bartolini Legacy duet,
check out

The Prince and the Wedding Planner

And look out for the next book
Coming soon!

If you enjoyed this story,
look out for these other great reads from
Jennifer Faye

Her Christmas Pregnancy Surprise
Wearing the Greek Millionaire's Ring
Claiming the Drakos Heir
Carrying the Greek Tycoon's Baby

All available now!